Taken by Two

BY SAM J.D. HUNT

Chapter One   D.4-16

He sat at the onyx granite bar slowly circling the rim of his crystal tumbler with his long finger. I couldn't take my eyes off him. Nathaniel Slater—the man of my dreams. There was a time when we moved in the same circles, had friends in common, knew each other in passing. Well, at least that's what he would probably say. To me, he was the guy I sat up nights scheming over—*how could I get him to notice me?* That was before—before he disappeared over a year ago.

I sipped my chardonnay, blatantly staring at the fascinating Nathaniel Slater. He was new money; a rich dot-com billionaire type who'd made a name for himself with video conferencing software. My family, in contrast, was very old money. My father, David Sedgewick, was from a long line of Northeast blue bloods. Grandmother could trace our family line back to the Mayflower and beyond.

I continued to stare. His finger paused its circling long enough for him to wrap his palm around the glass and take a slow sip of the amber liquid. I slid off my stool, wine glass in hand, and made my way toward him. "If I didn't know better, I'd swear you were back from the dead," I whispered at his silver-suited shoulder. He savored one last unhurried sip before taking a deep breath and turning his gaze toward me. "No idea what you're talking about. Great pickup line, though." His steel-blue eyes locked on to mine; a cold shiver tap-danced down my spine. He was beautiful, and right there with me. "Penny Sedgewick," he said, his tongue wrapping around the vowels as if savoring them as he'd done the bourbon.

"The one and only," I replied. The man I'd always wanted sat right there in my favorite bar, the exclusive Taster's Club, at *my* casino—well, my father's casino, really. He'd named one of his mega resort casinos on the Las Vegas Strip after me—*The Penelope*. My manicured nails pushed back my long blonde hair as my red lips parted in a smile. "Pleased to make your acquaintance, Mr…?"

His pink lips curled at the edges in a wry smile. "Nice to meet you, Penny. Care to join me?" Nathaniel gestured toward the empty stool at his side. My red silk dress was tight around my ample curves, but I managed to gracefully slide up next to him as he took my hand. With two fingers he gestured to the bartender for another round.

"So, you didn't disappear into the murky Amazon River then?"

"I'm afraid you have me mistaken for someone else, Miss Sedgewick. My name is Jason

King and I'm in Vegas for a life insurance convention." His copper eyelashes fluttered over his mesmerizing blue-gray eyes as his pink tongue swiped across his full lips. The suit he wore was a tailored Armani, probably made for him. The shoes were Italian leather and finer than the pricey red designer stiletto pumps hanging from my own pedicured feet. As I leaned in to take another long sip of my too-warm chardonnay, I could smell his cologne. It was masculine, imported, and very expensive. Clearly Nathaniel Slater didn't care to discuss his disappearance from social life, but he did seem attracted to me. His leg drifted to the left until his thigh was touching my own.

With a warm smile, he slid my new glass toward me. "That one has lost its chill," he said. "Allow me to replace your wine." I pushed the old glass aside and reached for the new one, the top covered with his hand as if he didn't want to let it go. "Cheers," he said, placing his left hand on my thigh before throwing back the glass of bourbon. I took a hard gulp of the cold wine, eager to feel the subtle buzz that would give me the courage to take him up to my penthouse suite. As I took another sip, I began to feel tipsy. By the third slurp, I was drunk.

"Odd," I said too loudly as he stared at me, his hands raking through his dark auburn brown hair.

"What is, Penny?"

"I-I don't normally, I mean alcohol doesn't…"

That was the last thing I remember about that night.

What seemed like days later, I could hear them talking before I could manage to open my eyes. My heavy eyelids fluttered, struggled to rise, then gave up and left me lying in the darkness. I wasn't uncomfortable or in any pain, but the heavy stupor of confusion sent me back to the black fog of sleep. Under the curtain of my induced slumber, I lived vivid dreams. In one, a burly man, tattooed, muscled, and strong, was speaking to me in a deep voice, reassuring me that everything was going to be fine as long as I obeyed.

Eventually my eyes finally managed to part enough that I could see where I was. The room was dimly lit and vibrating in an off-putting way—as if the bed where I lay was on top of an enormous engine. *An airplane*, I thought, *I'm on a private jet.* I was no stranger to luxurious travel—I'd been on planes like this one many times. Rolling out of bed, I crawled over to the door. My legs felt rubbery, as if they lacked the strength to support me. The thin door wasn't locked. Nathaniel Slater had to have kidnapped me—I vaguely remembered him nearly carrying my limp body from the club—explaining to the bartender, who worked for my father, that he was taking me back to my room to sleep it off. I couldn't remember anything else, but Hank, the bartender, wouldn't have questioned Nathaniel's claim. I wasn't known to drink to excess, but I *was* known to take handsome men back up to my suite.

The light from the main cabin hurt my eyes. A large man, the man from my dream, was sitting in a cream-colored leather chair with his back to me. Nathaniel sat on the floor next to the large man, his head in his hands. He still wore the silver suit pants, but the jacket and tie were gone. The wave of his silky brown hair cascaded over his splayed fingers. The other man, his hair a dark blonde caramel-like color, was wearing worn jeans that clung to his muscular thighs. His legs were long—so long that he had to be at least six foot seven, maybe taller. The jeans ended in heavy black leather boots—motorcycle or combat boots, possibly. The man's powerful arms were covered in tattoos.

"I still don't get why you took her, Nate. I mean, what the *fuck* were you thinking?" The husky grit of his low voice pierced the silence as his fingers tensed on the arm of the chair in frustration, or maybe fury. The idea of Nathaniel kidnapping me was terrifying, but my real fear sprang from the ominous man in the chair.

"I-I don't know, Rex, I'm sorry. But what was I supposed to do—just leave her *there?*"

"You were supposed to do what you were told, Nate. You fucking tricked me!" His fist slammed down on the side of the chair, causing Nate to flinch.

"I'm sorry," Nate said so quietly I could barely hear him.

And then…he leaned into the monstrous man, Rex, and rested his head on Rex's muscled thigh. I leaned back on my heels—*the gesture was so intimate.*

"It's okay, I'll figure it out. I'm just afraid of any complications that will put you at risk. And *she* is definitely a complication." Rex's fingers reached down and ran through Nate's hair before resting across his back.

My legs were going numb from my weight on them. As I moved to shift the weight, my groggy body toppled over and fell to the plane's floor in a thud as I drifted back into sleep.

"Wake up, Penny." Nathaniel Slater was next to me on the bed, wiping a cold cloth across my forehead.

"What…ah…please don't hurt me," I begged as I finally came to. "I don't know who you are, I don't know anything. Just let me go."

He shook his head in pity. "I'd never hurt you, Penny. Do exactly as Rex says and you'll be fine. I drugged you at the bar—but I needed to. I had to have you with us. I'm sorry the after-effects are hitting you harder than most. Can you drink some water?"

He lifted me until I sat up in the bed, my back against a padded leather headboard. "Where are we going?" He held a bottle of water to my lips and ignored my question until I'd drank enough to satisfy him. He wrapped his arm around me and pulled me close. I knew I should resist, but instead I crumpled into his embrace. At the moment, he seemed like the only friend I had. "We're going home," he answered simply.

His pale eyes swept across my face—his fingertips tentatively brushed across my cheek. "I've always thought you were so beautiful, Penny. I remember when you were dating that jerk Clyde. I wanted to get to know you, but we just never seemed to be in the right place at the right time. Then when I saw you sitting across the bar, I knew it was all going to be just as it should."

I was shocked—I didn't realize Nathaniel Slater even noticed me back then. "Clyde was a giant mistake," I mused, remembering the humiliation he'd put me through. "But holy fuck, Nathaniel!" He swiped my bottom lip with his finger, unfazed by my freak-out. "You can call me Nate." I sighed, fighting my attraction to him to *think*. "Nate, let me get this straight—you *kidnapped* me to get to know me? I'm flattered, but that's really messed up." His face reddened as if I'd slapped his cheek. "Kidnapped? Oh my God, no! I took you to keep you safe." He took a deep breath and pulled me against him again, his face close to mine, the smell of his cologne causing me to stir despite my brain scolding my libido that this was no game. "I want to go home, back to Vegas, now," I said, trying to sound assertive. With a sigh, he answered, "Can't do that, babe. Even if I wanted to, it's too dangerous now. We're already almost to the compound. You've been sleeping for hours."

"Hours?" He nodded in response. I felt like I'd been out for days, not hours.

"The other guy, Rex," I whispered, "does he have you captured, too?"

Nathaniel chuckled. "Rex? Nah, he'd never keep me against my will. I *want* to be with him—he saved my life."

"Saved you from the Amazon?"

He shook his head, but stayed silent.

"Are you related? Or…lovers?" I couldn't help but ask as I thought back to Rex's fingers gliding through Nate's hair.

With a snort, he answered, "No and no. You're big into labels, aren't you?"

His eyes warmed as he leaned in, his nose brushing against the tip of mine. "I'll keep you safe, Penny. Rex won't let anything happen to you, either. He's rough on the outside, but he's not a bad guy. But, he *is* dangerous, so trust me and do what he says and we *might* just get out of this alive."

I was afraid of the dark Rex—and drawn to the exquisite Nate. I rolled toward him, my lips kissing his neck. "I won't force you to do anything, Penny," he sighed as I rolled on top of him. His erection ground against the silken fabric of my dress as his lips parted for my tongue. "I've wanted you since the moment I saw you," I confessed as my hands slid down to toy with the bulge of his hardness. If I was about to die a horrific death, I may as well cross an item off my bucket list. *Fuck Nathaniel Slater, check.* And, I felt like I really needed Nate on my side against the scary, tattooed giant.

The slick suit pants fell away as I clawed at his clothing, desperate to free him. With a sharp tug, the zipper down my back opened, allowing him to pull me from the confines of the dress. We gracelessly pawed at clothing until we were skin to skin, writhing across each other like two teenagers after a school dance. "*Are you sure?*" he moaned into my mouth, his fingers pressing at my entrance, working their way inside me. "*Yes, I want you,*" I groaned in response, my fingertips stroking his tip, teasing the delicate ridge just underneath.

Our tongues found each other, their sensual dance silencing us as we kissed—a kiss like none I'd ever known. He stroked my clit, the bundle of nerves near explosion as the sweet tension built. *"I'm desperate for you,"* I begged as my hand wrapped around the throbbing flesh of his thick cock.

Strong arms flipped me over as he rolled on top of me. His warm lips found my hard nipples—so sensitive I howled in ecstasy as he sucked hard on one of them. *"Oh, fuck,"* I yelled, not caring that Rex might hear—not caring about anything but giving and receiving pleasure—as his impossibly hard cock sank deep inside me, scraping against my cervix in a thrust so deep I thought he'd tear me in two.

"Shit, Penny, you're so perfect and tight." The pad of his thumb brushed across my sensitive bundle of nerves. As my hips thrust against him, he rubbed harder on my clit. I exploded around him as he fucked me, oblivious to anything but us. Oblivious, that is, until I slowly recovered from the intensity of my climax—and saw *him* lurking there.

Nate continued to pound into me—fucking me like he hadn't touched a woman in years; fucking me like a starving man at a buffet. I froze, unable to speak underneath him. Rex stood in the shadows of the entryway, leaning casually against the doorframe. His hands were stuffed into the pockets of his worn jeans as he stood motionless, watching us. Shocked and afraid, I tried to push Nate off, but he wouldn't budge. The force of his thrusts never relented inside me; I could tell he was close to coming.

"He's watching us," I hissed into Nate's deliciously scented ear.

His eyes fluttered open, the pace pausing briefly. "Huh? Oh, it's okay, Penny. He said I could."

His rhythm increased again, despite my fingernails clawing into his back. After he shuddered in a powerful climax, filling me, I whispered, "He said you could *what?*" He panted, his toned chest still heaving from the effort of his release, and answered, "Rex gave me permission to have you."

I was horrified. *Was I stolen as a sex slave? Or did they intend to rape me and...* The thought was too terrible. I pushed at his chest; I wanted him off me. My eyes shot to the doorway; Rex was gone. Nate rolled off me, a look of concern flooding his face. "Penny, what is it? I-I thought you wanted... What did I do wrong?" His tone was soft, genuine. I relaxed as his fingertips brushed gingerly across my cheek. The steel-blue eyes were filled with concern. I was confused; unsure of what was real and what I was imagining. "Why did you take me? Is Rex going to kill me?"

He shook his head, his eyes narrowing. "God, no, we'd never...I took you to keep you safe. I admit I hoped we might, um, hit it off, and that Rex would like you, too. Earlier he said if you wanted me, if we...he said it was okay if we were together."

That was twisted, my groggy brain screamed. "Let me go!'

"I can't. I'm sorry—I can't explain. You were in danger in Vegas. When the danger is over, we'll take you home." He turned his face to mine; his hypnotic blue eyes locking on my brown ones as his palm cradled my chin. "I'll take care of you, I promise." I shouldn't have, but I believed him. I fell asleep on Nate's lean, muscular chest, naked and leaking his essence as we drifted off to sleep.

The next morning, the soft awareness of awakening floated over me—my eyes were still closed, but the fugue of the drug Nate used on me was gone. I felt like myself again—and couldn't help but let my hand wander over to the sexy Nathaniel Slater lying next to me. As my palm wandered across him, I skimmed a hard, clothed being. My eyes popped open in a startle.

"Good morning, Princess. Was it good for you, too?" The scary man, Rex, was sitting next to me in bed—wearing the same dark t-shirt, worn jeans, and even the heavy black boots. *Combat boots*, I thought as my confused brain fought to form a plan. His muscled arm reached across me, the thick pattern of tattoos ended just above his wrist. "What—um, where's Nate?" He chuckled and groped at my sheet in an attempt to pull it off me—I fought back and yanked it with both hands. He relented, but we both knew he was strong enough to do as he pleased with me. Rex was a huge, hulking presence—his menacing midnight blue eyes raked over my exposed skin.

"I sent him home ahead of us to prepare."

"Does he always obey you?" The man nodded.

"Did you capture him like you did me?" I was terrified, but determined to keep my wits.

He cracked his knuckles and stared at me. I wasn't sure if it was a threat, but it felt very much like a warning. "Everyone obeys me here, Princess. I'm the king on this island—King Rex." He laughed out loud, his enormous barrel chest rising and falling underneath the cotton of his t-shirt. He was toying with me, and enjoying it. "Besides, I didn't capture

11

you, baby. Nathaniel did. In fact, your presence here is pretty much fucking up everything right now." He leaned over and wrapped his immense hand around my throat and squeezed in warning. "So behave, or I'll fucking toss you to the snakes, Princess."

My hands shot up to my constricted neck, desperate to loosen his grasp as I struggled to breathe. "Are we clear?" His fingers effortlessly pulsed once more around my tortured throat before letting go. "Yes," I coughed. "Yes, what?" He flexed his fingers as if he were going to choke me again. "Yes, Rex?" He rubbed at his knuckles and sighed, as if I'd failed my first test. "Yes, sir, would be nice. But I guess I'll allow you to call me Rex. Now get up, we're home. *My* home, not yours," he said, pointing a long index finger at me. "Yes, sir," I answered, my throat still raw from his strong hand.

The golden daylight was streaming into the small cabin of the airplane—dust particles danced in the bright rays of sun. The engine had shut down, and an eerie silence hung over the room. "Well, get dressed," he croaked, pointing to my red silk dress on the floor across the cabin. I pulled the sheet around me and began to rise from the bed, but he yanked at it again. "Leave the sheet—and walk over and get dressed. *Slowly*."

He'd spied on Nate and me having sex hours prior, but this seemed even more horrific. It was daylight, and he was fully dressed. With an amused smirk he added, "And do it now, or I'll toss your sexy, curvy body over my shoulder and take you to my compound bare-ass naked." I looked into his eyes— they weren't angry, but slightly annoyed and very amused. He licked his lips in anticipation as I slid out from under the crisp linen sheet. Completely naked, I walked across the carpeted floor of the private airplane toward my crumpled dress. I bent down and snagged my panties while formulating a plan to manipulate the coarse, behemoth kidnapper. I didn't even know if a man like Rex would find me attractive, but I'd found many men still loved curves and, despite not being built like a model, I knew how to work my Burlesque-like sensuality. As I bent at the waist, I let my full breasts hang heavily until I stood up again. I pulled the lace panties on one leg at a time as I looked over toward Rex. The change in him was palpable. The amusement was gone; replaced with a look I recognized—lust. A glance to his jeans confirmed it— the smug Rex's erection strained not to bust through the soft fabric of his well-fitting jeans.

"You can skip the bra," he groaned, resting the palm of his hand across his bulging erection.

"They're fairly heavy, sir, may I?" I asked, reaching for my lace bra. He nodded, a fine dew of sweat glistening on his tanned forehead. Men may *think* they have the power, but I have my weapons— even against dominant alpha males like Rex.

I wrapped the lace bra around my weighty triple-D breasts before reaching for the silk dress. He was attracted to me—he shifted on the bed, his desire for me a tangible presence in the snug cabin. Stepping into the dress, I turned my back to him. "Zip me, sir?" I waited—praying he'd take the bait. Within seconds I heard his heavy feet shuffle toward me, his rough fingers deftly pulling the zipper up my back.

He grabbed me—his strong arms wrapping around my round waist. "Don't play with me, Penny." Continuing to hold me, his breathing was ragged, his erect cock pressing against my lush ass. *He used my name*, I thought, a smile fighting its way to my lips.

I ground against him before walking a step to slide into my designer pumps. I turned to face him. Rex was big—not just tall, but built like a tank. He towered over me, his hands stuffed in his jeans pockets—his prominent hard cock forming an immense curved outline against his torso. *Damn, Nathaniel is beautiful, but this guy is all sexy testosterone*, I thought as he walked toward me.

I moved to lean into him, to flirt, but he grabbed me hard and yanked me toward the door. "Let's go," he barked as I fought to stay upright on my stilettos. He was several feet behind me as we walked through the opulent interior of the small jet. I knew this was my chance to escape—there was no way this ape was taking me to his *compound*, no matter how sexy he was. The second it was within reach, I sprinted toward the cockpit and slammed the door behind me—in Rex's face, I realized, as I felt the impact of flesh and heard him swear. Locking it, I quickly begged the two uniformed men to help me. "Please, I've been kidnapped, I'm Penelope Sedgewick and I…" Neither man moved. One looked to the other, hands flying up in a question, and said simply, "Que?" The other man looked from his co-pilot to me, but made no effort to move. "Please! Help me!" I begged of the man who seemed to understand English. "It's okay, Miguel," he said to his co-pilot. "Miss, open the door. Mr. Renton is going to be pissed as fuck." I was incredulous as he stood and brushed past me in the cramped cockpit, opening the heavy door.

Rex stood there, his hand wiping blood away from his nose. *Shit!* "Do you need me to help you contain her, sir?" Rex walked toward the pilot, *his* pilot, I now realized, shaking his head. "Nah, this little impertinent brat is going to learn a fucking lesson," he boomed as he grabbed me by the arm. Shaking with fear—calculating in my always scheming brain what to do next—I let him pull me from the cockpit and down the narrow stairs to the hot tarmac.

"What the fuck was that? *Everyone* here works for me—I don't want to hurt you, Penny!" He was talking under his breath as he dragged me toward a large dark van. The humidity of the locale, some tropical island possibly, wrapped around me and caused the silk dress to cling to my body. "I thought you *did* want to hurt me, Rex, I mean you've choked me and now—"

"I'm the one who's bleeding here, lady! I gave you a little frisky throat hug, nothing more, just to remind you of your manners. I'm not a caveman, though—I'd rather not harm you. But, I will if it means keeping Nate safe, do you understand? I'll do *anything* to keep him from harm." He pushed me from behind into the interior of the van—a blast of frigid air taking my breath away as he climbed in behind me. "You captured Nate, though, you…" Rex sighed heavily—I can be exasperating under the best of circumstances. I'm sure I didn't make the best captive. "I didn't capture Nate, for fuck's sake! He captured me."

Chapter Two

The windows of the van were completely blacked out—I had no clue where he was taking me. I sat across the chilly van from Rex and watched him tap on his cell phone, a Blackberry—the tiny device almost comical looking in his large hands. His long legs were spread wide as he hunched over, tapping out some message with his large thumbs. On his left ring finger he wore a heavy gold band—I stared at it, trying to learn as much as I could about the enemy.

The thin silk dress didn't offer me any protection against the blasting air conditioning of the van. "Rex," I said, "I'm freezing—can we turn down the A/C? Or maybe can I borrow a jacket?" I used my softest tone of voice, but his dark eyes bore into me, his nose crinkled in a sneer. "Please, sir," I added, suspecting I wasn't on his good side. "I'm hot," he said slowly, his eyes returning to his phone. My arms wrapped around my torso, shivering as I hunched into the vinyl seat.

He looked up and sighed before banging his hand on the divider glass separating us from the driver. It slid down, and a dark skinned man, perhaps Hispanic, answered, "Yes, Mr. Renton?" Rex pointed at me. "Rodrigo, can you turn the air down—the pampered Princess here is cold." The driver reached over and with a stab of a button the strong wind of frigid air stopped. "Thank you, that's all." The glass slid back up.

"Thanks," I said, still chilled but relieved to not be shaking.

"Here," he croaked, reaching toward his waist and pulling his dark t-shirt up over his torso. "It's all I have. We're about fifteen minutes away. I think I have some chick clothes stashed somewhere you can wear—although I'd rather that flawless body stay naked." His large cotton t-shirt landed on my lap, but I was too distracted to bother wrapping it around my goose-bumped arms. Rex's abs were more than a six-pack, they were an eight-pack if that even exists. A light dusting of dark blonde hair covered his perfectly defined pecs, the line going down his center—my lusty eyes drank in his toned, inked body. Most distracting was his right nipple—a metal barbell piercing ran through it. I stared until he cleared his throat, drawing me back to reality. "Distracted, Princess?" A flirty smile slid across his lips. He winked and went back to his Blackberry, the knowing smile still visible at the edges of his lips.

I pulled his t-shirt over my arms as a warm blush rose from my chest to my cheeks. Yes, he'd caught me looking—but who wouldn't look? The man was physical perfection and, even sexier, the cotton of his shirt smelled like all man. His scent was spicy and virile, with nothing artificial to cover up his masculinity. Nate smelled like a luscious cologne, but Rex smelled like an alpha male to die for.

A few minutes later, Rex broke the silence by answering his vibrating phone. "What's up, man?" he said casually. His eyes looked over at me as he said, "Yeah, we're ten minutes out." He listened to the caller before answering, "Uh, yeah, I have it—I'll get it done one way or another." He ended the call and said to me, "Want some water?" My mouth was dry and gummy—I hadn't had anything to drink for hours. "God, yes, I'm parched, my mouth is like sandpaper." He reached into a compartment at the side of the van and pulled out a bottle of Fiji-brand water. I licked my dry lips, relieved that he was treating me civilly. He twisted the blue cap off and drained the entire bottle into his gulping throat. When he finished, he let a little roll down his scruffy chin before crushing the bottle in the palm of his hand. "Behave, and when you get to your room, you can have a drink. Maybe water, maybe…" He winked at me again and wiped the water from his face with the back of his hand.

I felt the chill of a cold sweat—Rex was clearly the type of man who had a sadistic streak; he liked to toy with a captive. Whether he would really hurt me or not, I wasn't sure. Despite my trepidation, the thought of him coating my tongue betrayed me—my clit swelling and throbbing as we pulled into an industrial type garage.

The van came to a stop, but the large doors on the side didn't open. Rex put his phone in his pocket and turned to face me, leaning in as if he was about to deliver bad news. "Listen, Penelope," his voice was deep, serious. He'd never used my full first name before. A tremor ran across my spine. "I need you to get in this bag, it'll only be for a—"

"No, please, I beg you—I won't, I can't, don't…" He was reaching into a storage compartment and pulling out a body-sized burlap bag. "Don't kill me!" I howled. His eyes narrowed as his eyebrows knitted together. "What? No, I'm not going to… I can't have you seeing my place. Slip into the sack and I'll carry you to your room. Behave and I'll take care of you, fight me and I'll toss you into the pond with the reptiles."

"Blindfold me, anything but a bag. I-I'm claustrophobic, I can't…"

"Sorry, Princess." He leaned over in the cramped van and grabbed me, yanking me to the floor. I fought as he leaned his weight on me, holding me in place against the rough carpeted floor. "Be still," he threatened as I continued to writhe and flail against his hard body. My mind went back to when I was seven; I accidentally got locked in a broken freezer in a friend's garage. We were playing hide and seek, but once I got in, I couldn't get out. They didn't find me for almost an hour—and to this day I fear enclosed, dark places—that and anything that slithered.

My knee moved to sink into Rex's groin, but before I made contact his fingers dug into a nerve in my neck—I was paralyzed, frozen there at his mercy.

"You're alright," his deep voice crooned, rough but I could tell he was attempting to calm me. I should have been able to speak, but for some reason the feeling of being immobilized by his fingers on some sort of pressure point shocked me into silence.

The dark fabric covered my face, and he quickly pulled it around me and held me in his arms like a baby. "*Please*," I begged from the darkness of the bag. He didn't answer, but he held me tighter— the sensation more cradling than rough. He was walking quickly, the steamy humid heat replacing the cool, dry air of the van. Voices surrounded us, speaking what I thought was Spanish—or maybe Italian. Rex's low baritone answered them fluently, in their language, as he continued to walk briskly with me in his arms.

In a few moments we were indoors again—the sensation of an artificially cooled area was unmistakable, even inside the cloth sack. Another short few moments passed, and I was being placed gently on a bed. After a loud click, Rex pulled the sack up over my feet and legs as I wiggled out of the bag.

As my eyes opened, my chest heaving from fear, Rex hovered over me, his body resting on the bed beside me. I looked into his eyes—searching for some sort of reassurance that I would make it home alive. "You okay?" he husked, his hands brushing the hair from my eyes. "Uh huh, I think so…" I finally managed to squeak out. "I'll get you some water," he said absently as his fingertips brushed against my cheek. "The door is locked from the outside. I don't know you yet, Princess—I don't trust easily.

Nathaniel bringing you with us has put all of us in danger." I nodded, even though I had no idea what he was talking about. His combination of hard and soft, warm and cold, kept me on edge.

The door locked behind him. I looked around the room—it was a normal bedroom, and there was sunlight coming from the two windows. They were covered in heavy bars, but other than that, the room didn't seem like a prison, but more like a guest room. Well, like a barred guest room that locked from the outside. As messed up as it was, I yearned for Nate. He felt safe and comfortable, despite Rex's reminding me that Nate actually was my captor. *Rex must have brainwashed Nate*, I reasoned.

Rex returned with a small basket and a duffle bag, and my lusty eyes weren't disappointed that he was still shirtless. He opened the basket and pulled out a bottle of water, pointing it toward me. I greedily sipped the cool liquid as he watched me. "Hungry?" He held out a sandwich, but I shook my head. "Come on, Nate said you needed to eat. He made it with his own two lovely hands." The mention of Nate perked me up. "Can I see him? He's here?"

"Not yet. He'll be in to see you if you can manage to behave."

"I'm a prisoner then." I looked around the room.

"No, these are precautions. I have to detain you for now, that's all."

I nodded, unconvinced.

"Eat, drink, and relax. There's a TV over in the armoire—it's not connected to the outside world, but there's a shitload of movies there in the drawer.

That door," he said, pointing to the side of the room, "is your bathroom. This bag has some women's clothing—I'm not sure they'll fit, but you won't be here long." He stood up and headed for the door as I slunk into the bed.

Halfway to the door, he turned and said aloud, "Oh, I almost forgot." In a flash, he lunged at me, his heavy body crushing mine against the mattress.

"Stop!" I screamed, horrified that he "almost forgot" to attack me. This man was insane, insane *and* violent.

"You are so damn feisty!" he howled, scrambling for something in his pockets.

In seconds he had my dress pulled up to my waist, and his large hands were yanking my panties down over my butt. "No, don't!" I begged, sure he was going to rape me.

"Be still," he said calmly as I felt a sharp jab.

Not a sexual jab, but a needle directly in the muscle of my behind.

"What was that?" I howled as he released me, pulling my panties up.

"Just a little shot to make sure you do as I say, Princess. Sorry to mar that perfect ass, though." He turned and left, leaving me sobbing on the bed.

Hours later, after several movies, Nate came in with a tray of food and an apologetic look. "Sorry I left you like that. Rex said to give you a few hours alone."

"Why?"

"I don't know," he shook his head and shrugged his shoulders.

"So you just did what he said without even asking—"

"Yes, Penny. I do what Rex tells me to do, without question." *Brainwashed.* The psychotic goon was controlling the sexy, beautiful, and perfect Nathaniel Slater. I mean, he was a hot as hell goon, but still.

"Nate," I sighed, "he's evil! He choked me, and then he injected me with some drug—"

"Don't say that!" He shook his head and stood up, heading toward the door.

"Wait, I'm sorry—don't leave me, *please.*"

He stopped and turned toward me. "I like you Penny, *a lot*, but I won't have you disrespecting Rex. He means the world to me. Whatever he's done, it's for our safety. Rex protects me, and he'll protect you, too. But you *must* obey him."

"Okay, okay, got it. Sit with me please? I'm so lonely and afraid." He nodded and walked over toward the small table where he'd set the tray of food. "Let's eat. Would you like some wine?" I was relieved when Nate popped the cork on a bottle of expensive chardonnay and poured two glasses before cuddling up next to me in the fluffy bed.

I tried to get physical with Nate, but he shook me off and explained, "Rex said I could only cuddle with you this time." I couldn't believe the level of mind-control the villain Rex had on my sweet Nate. I ran my fingers through his silky waves, the reddish brown color a sharp contrast to his flawless porcelain skin. My palm swept under his shirt; the feel of his ripped chest and the perfect V of his abs tying my greedy clit into knots. He lovingly pulled my fingers back as his cock swelled, muttering a gentle, "Not now, babe." Unable to seduce him, we dozed off to sleep in a wine buzz with some romantic comedy playing out on the large television from a DVD we'd popped in earlier. I slept soundly in Nate's comforting embrace—despite haunting worries of what sort of drug the evil Rex had injected me with.

When I woke up, it was morning and Nate was gone. I wandered into the small bathroom—an assortment of toiletries was lined up on the counter. The one small window, like the ones in my room, was barred. I took a shower, crying as I washed my hair. Thoughts of my father flooded me—my mom died three years ago, and despite a long estrangement, I'd grown closer to my father. He had to know I was gone, and I prayed he was looking for me.

I brushed my teeth with the new toothpaste and toothbrush on the sink before blow-drying my long blonde hair. *Think Penelope*, I scolded myself as I washed my face. I looked through the drawers—no makeup. Even though he was the one who kidnapped me, I sensed that Nate was my chance at freedom—his soft, warm presence was my best hope for escape. He was clearly brainwashed by the cruel King Rex, but he was also falling for me. Even without lipstick and eyeliner, I had to win over Nate.

When I emerged from the bathroom, the TV was off. Rex sat in a chair at the side of the room, tapping at his Blackberry. He was wearing darker jeans than the day prior, just as strained over his muscled legs, the same black combat boots, and a green camouflage t-shirt that struggled to cover his bulging biceps. He never looked up at me as I sat on the edge of the bed. We sat silently for what seemed like forever before he finally slid the phone in his pocket and looked up at me.

"Ah, you look nice, Princess. Much better with the war paint washed off." His eyes roamed across my body. "The clothes fit?"

"A little snug, but yeah, they'll do. Whose were they?"

A curtain of sadness slid across his face. "None of your fucking business," he snapped. His large chest filled with air, and he slowly exhaled. He was trying to control his temper. "Listen, sweetheart, I'm here to chat with you because Nate the Kindhearted begged me to, and well, he can be quite…*persuasive*."

"If you let me go, I won't tell anyone, I swear. Just drop me back in the States. I mean, they'll be looking for me."

He shook his head. "No one's looking for ya, baby." His dark stare bore into me.

"The bartender at my father's club *saw* Nate leave with me, he'll—"

An arrogant smirk slid across his lips. "No, sweetheart, they think you willingly left with a handsome ex-boyfriend for an extended frolic on the French Riviera. And as far as the bartender, well—I *took care* of him."

I gasped. Hank had been a friend of mine for years, my confidant at the club where I practically lived every evening. "You didn't!" I whispered as the tears sprung to my eyes.

"Penny—I assure you that Henry Joseph Harrington, bartender of five years, who lives at 2344

Desert Crest in Boulder City, Nevada isn't going to save you. *No one* cares, *no one* is looking for you."

I began to sob—I knew he was right. I had few friends and I'd burned through my family fairly fast after the calming presence of my mother was gone. My father tried—he loved me in his own way—but his business and new wife were his priorities, and I was left to my own devices.

I hated the mean King Rex Renton at that moment. Despite my glare, his deep voice began to speak again. "So, Princess, I have a business matter I have to attend to. I'll be gone for a bit, and I've commanded Nate to not see you until I return. Maria will take good care of you—*if* you behave. Give her trouble, and I've given her permission to dump you into the croc pit. Are we clear?"

"Yeah," I answered through my sniffles.

"Excuse me?" He stood and walked in front of me, his dark presence hovering over me, his massive fists balled in a threat.

"Yes, sir," I sniffled.

"Better."

"What did you inject me with yesterday?" I asked softly.

"Just something to ensure you behave, that's all." His large index finger pointed an inch from my face, "I don't have the time or the energy for complications, Penny. Not *even* for Nate." He left the room, the harsh metallic click of the lock on the other side reminding me of how helpless I was.

By lunchtime, my stomach was growling. A dark haired woman finally opened the door with a nod. She set down a tray covered in linen cloth, and in slow, trained English asked, "Do you need anything, Miss?"

I nodded. "I need to leave."

"I cannot," she said as she left.

I spent the next two days alone in the artificially cooled room. I was fed, but Maria spoke very little English. After dinner the second evening, I lay in a heap on the plush carpeted floor, sobbing and feeling sorry for myself. I was jolted from my self-indulgent cry by the opening of my bedroom door. I expected to see the dark-haired maid, but instead my heart began to pound when I recognized the tall, lean frame of Nate as he slid the door closed behind him, locking it from the inside with a key that he placed in the pocket of his slim jeans.

"Penny," he cooed as he knelt down beside me. "Don't cry, I'm so sorry."

He held me tight, rocking me in his arms. "You left me," I wailed.

"Rex said I couldn't see you until he returned. I tried, but I missed you so damn much." He leaned in and kissed me, his warm lips caressing mine.

"I tried," he purred, wrapping my limbs around his. "I meant to stay away until Rex got home, but I'm drawn to you. I-I've never felt like this about a woman before."

My lips found his again, silencing his explanations, his apology. At that moment, my yearning wasn't for escape; it was for him. My tongue caressed his, the need flowing from me as he unbuttoned my shirt. "*You're so beautiful,*" he moaned as his lips dipped down to kiss the very top of the lace of my bra. My full breasts heaved over the top of the cups—whoever owned this exquisite bra was smaller breasted than me. His eager fingers pulled the lace aside, the ivory flesh flowing over the strained fabric.

His full lips wrapped around my sensitive pink nipple, his desperate suction so intense I struggled to bear it. "Nate," I begged, clawing at the fly of his jeans. He released the aroused nipple and stood, reaching out a hand to pull me up and toward the bed. We fell together against the pillows, struggling to free one another of the oppressive clothing that separated us.

As his gloriously swollen cock burst free of his jeans, I wrapped my lips around it, drawing hard as he writhed against the sheets. "Pen, wait, not so fast..." I stroked his firm, swollen balls with my index finger, slowing my rhythm on his long shaft as he pulled at me. He managed to flip me over, despite my pout at being parted from his hardness.

"I need to taste you first..."

My tongue was salty from the liquid that slowly seeped from him as he dipped his warm tongue into me—savoring and worshipping me in the most intimate way he could. A long finger slid into my tightness as he lapped at me, so gently I yearned for more. My hips rose as my fingers combed through his thick hair—pressing him into me. His tongue picked up speed as I pushed against his mouth—silently begging him for more contact. *"You are so sweet,"* he purred against my throbbing sex. When he flicked at my clit with the very tip of his tongue, his fingertip pressing against the sponginess of my swollen G-spot, I struggled to stay quiet as my orgasm rocked me. Nate rode it out, not letting go despite my efforts to shake him loose. He greedily held on to sip every last drop of sweetness from me before rising to take me in his arms.

His tongue found mine once again, sharing my own slick essence from his mouth to mine. My fingers slid down to hold onto his hard shaft, stroking it slowly until he could take no more.

"I'm going to die if I can't be inside you soon," he begged as my thighs fell open to allow him to plunge deep inside me.

I screamed as his thickness parted me, despite his hand covering my mouth in a vain attempt to quiet me.

My nails clawed into his back as he thrust—hard and unyielding against my tightness—over and over until we both shuddered in climatic ecstasy.

I fell asleep with Nate, perfect and beautiful, wrapped around me. Irrationally, I didn't want to leave him. But the big guy, Rex, scared me shitless. He had complete control over Nate—brainwashed, clearly. *And what if what he injected me with was some sort of drug that would make me the same way?* No, I had to stop pretending as if I were in some sweeping adventure novel and get the fuck off that island before shit got real.

The more I thought about it, the more freaked out I became. *This isn't a game,* I thought, my heart pounding. *These men could kill me...* I slid from the bed and found his jeans. Inside, there was the key he'd used to lock the door.

I managed to open the lock from the inside with his key—and after dressing in the snug borrowed clothes, I slinked from the bedroom that had become my jail cell and out into a modern living room.

Chapter Three

"Penny, what the fuck?" Strong arms were lifting me, carrying me—but my heavy eyelids wouldn't open, my parched lips were sealed shut. I'd been ridiculously unprepared for my attempt at escape, and ended up wandering the harsh jungle for hours and hours until I somehow tripped and fell. I don't remember where I landed, just being very thirsty and confused.

I'm not sure how far he carried me. In my dream-like state, I wasn't sure if I was alive or dead. My head pounded, my heart fluttered. Nate's angelic face floated by my thoughts, his steel blue eyes comforting as he called to me. Rex's deep voice vibrated from somewhere near, whether real or imagined, I'm still not sure. "Hang in there, baby girl, I've got you," he reassured me that afternoon.

It all went dark for a long time, and then a blinding light flooded my vision. My head was in a thick cloud, pounding and pained. The light burned, and yet his fingers were forcing my eyes open. "Penelope, say something."

I struggled to open my eyes. Rex was hovering over me, the unmistakable look of concern in his eyes betraying his normal coldness. "I–I got lost, I was thirsty, fell into the river…so chilly…" I shivered, despite the brutal humid heat of the jungle around us. A scratchy wool blanket was wrapped around me. It was dark—I managed to tilt my head—we were in a tent. A tiny tent; my escape plan had been an epic failure. *What would he do to me now?*

"You're dehydrated, suffering from exposure. Falling into the river probably saved your life, sweetheart." Rex's normally harsh voice was soft, deep and swaddling as he spoke, his fingers brushing across my forehead. "Good thing I gave you a typhoid shot."

"Shot?" I was beginning to awaken.

"The other day, in your room. The injection was a typhoid fever vaccine."

A cold cloth wiped over me, followed by cool water at my lips. "Drink a little more, sweetheart." I fell back into a sound, dream-filled sleep.

"I'll be okay?" I was awake again, after what seemed like hours of comatose sleep, and sitting up on a sleeping bag in the tiny tent. Rex sat across from me on the ground, his fingers raking through his hair. He nodded, his dark blue eyes rising to mine, a faint smile betraying his feigned anger.

"Tell me you didn't harm Nate." His words were icy cold, severe—he couldn't mask his concern for his—for Nate.

"I took the key from his jeans after we…"

"Why the fuck would you leave the compound? We're trying to keep you safe. You managed to escape from the good guys, Einstein, and almost got yourself killed in the process."

"I-I…I was kidnapped! You had me locked in a room against my will, then forcibly gave me a shot of something—oh yeah, and before that you stuck me in a canvas sack. And, of course, you *murdered* a friend of mine."

"What? *Murdered?*"

"The bartender you disposed of? I've known him for years." I couldn't believe I was arguing with a cold-blooded killer.

"I paid the guy off to not mention your leaving Vegas to have a tryst with some guy—I convinced him it would ruin the dude's trust fund and piss off his family. I didn't *hurt* your bartender."

"So you're not a killer?" I sniffed, struggling to understand it all with my dehydrated, fuzzy brain.

He relaxed, his hand wiping across my cheek. "Well, I wouldn't go that far. I didn't harm the bartender, anyway." He shook his head, and said with a grin, "You're such a pain in my ass." He gave me another sip of water, and said, "Ah, Penny, you have no idea the amount of trouble you've caused me today." He smiled at me despite his scolding words. "One more sip of water, then we'll try a little bit of Gatorade." He held the bottle to my lips tenderly.

"How many days have I been in this tent?" I wiped my lips as I looked around.

"All afternoon."

I was confused; surely I'd been floating in and out of consciousness for days. "That's all?" He chuckled again and nodded.

My head was pounding, my throat felt like I'd swallowed cotton. "I need a doctor," I begged.

He sat down on the sleeping bag next to me and pulled me into his arms. "I *am* a doctor, sweetheart."

When I awoke again, it was darker yet. The silver glow of moonlight illuminated the tent as I glanced around. Rex was next to me, my head on his chest. I sat up and debated whether I should run, but quickly abandoned the idea of escape. If Rex wanted to harm me, he wouldn't have spent all day nursing me back to health. He scared me, but I was beginning to understand him. He was far more bark than bite.

His eyelids popped open when he sensed my movement. I'd reached over to drink from a plastic bottle—the flat, sweet liquid tasting like heaven. "Little sips," he warned as he sat up. I nodded, setting the bottle back down. "I feel so much better. Can I go back?" He shook his head and looked at me with pity. "Penny, it's not safe for you to go back to Vegas. Right now, I can't even get you out of Colombia."

Colombia—we were in Colombia. That's not an island!

"Okay…" I believed him. "But can I go back to the house? It's not that far, right?"

"You wandered for miles, and I have a group of five men out there expecting to be led into the deep jungle to learn survival skills. They pay me a lot of money to teach them this shit. Looks like I have a new student." He poked me in the ribs. "I've already had to make up a story about who you are and why you are here—plus we've lost almost a whole day's trek while you recovered. I'll do my best to go easy on you, sweetheart, but welcome to hell."

After several more sips of Gatorade, Rex convinced me to sleep a few more hours until sunrise. As we lay back down together on the small sleeping bag, he offered, "If it gets too hard out there for you I'll call Nate to come get you when I get a signal. Try your best, though, Penny. I don't want Nate out here if I can avoid it—this group isn't the best crowd for him to be around—he's still vulnerable. The rest of the staff can't be trusted with you out here alone." *Vulnerable? To what?*

"Vulnerable," I repeated with a yawn. Suddenly, it all clicked. The physical intimacy between these two very alpha males, the level of trust Nate had in Rex, the protectiveness shown by Rex of Nate. *Nate must have some illness!* "*Oh*, you're his *doctor*," I said out loud.

Rex rolled over to face me in the pre-dawn blackness. "I swear, Princess, most of the time I have no idea what the actual fuck you're talking about. *Whose* doctor?"

"Nate's—I thought you might be lovers, but now I get it."

"*Lovers*—that's quite a ridiculous word. No, sweetheart, I'm not his *doctor*. Our relationship is far from a professional one, and none of your goddamn business. If you must know, I was once a field combat medic, but my *practice* quickly morphed into something much more…*classified*. Now go the fuck to sleep, or I *will* feed you to the snakes." The now-familiar threat of being tossed to reptiles, which had terrified me for days, I now realized was simply his twisted sense of humor. I refused to admit to him that my phobia of slithering creatures, especially snakes, was certifiable.

I wanted to ask more about Rex's past, and his relationship with Nate, but either he was fast asleep, or pretending to be in order to ignore me. Still processing the last few hours with this enigmatic man, I nudged up next to him, inhaling the manly scent I was beginning to like—like *a lot.*

"Morning, sunshine!" He was shaking me and yanking at the sleeping bag. "Get your lazy ass up, we're moving out." One of my eyes opened. Rex was hovering over me, agitated and threatening. "Now!" he hissed. His semi-sweet bedside manner from the night before had dissipated with the rising of the burning sun. "Yes, sir," I grumbled, sliding from the comfort of the covers.

He reached into a pocket and pulled out a tiny bar of something. "Breakfast," he said as he opened the crinkly wrapper. I reached out for it—I wasn't into granola bars, but I was starving. "We're sharing it, sweetheart. This is all the food we have until we catch lunch." He broke off a third of the bar and tossed it toward me. "You don't share so fairly," I mumbled as I chewed at the bland, dry cereal bar. "You're a third my size, you get a third—fair is fair. We could wrestle for it if you'd rather?" He winked at me as he devoured his share in two bites.

"Follow my lead out there—if word gets out that Penelope Sedgewick is here, we're all in trouble."

I nodded, rolling up the sleeping bag. "Where can I pee?" I asked sheepishly. My head still throbbed, but at least I finally had enough to drink that I needed to release it.

"I'll take you, but can you wait two secs while I pack up?"

In minutes, the tent and all of his belongings were packed into a heavy backpack. I was tossed a flimsy day-sack before he led me toward the group of campers. The anxious men hovered around us in a circle—staring. None of them spoke until Rex gestured to one of the younger ones. "Joe, can you start the guys walking—head due north. We'll catch up." He turned to me and pointed toward some tall vegetation near camp, "That way, *sis*."

"Sis?" I asked when the others were out of earshot. "I told them you were my step-sister, Joanie. After I found you yesterday, I quickly made up a story that my mom was staying with me and kicked you out into the jungle. I couldn't think of any other reason I'd have an unprepared woman out here." After walking several feet into the dense foliage, he pointed to a flattened area. "Sorry, no running water for you, Princess."

I was used to luxury, and had never camped out before, but I'd been known to party hard and squatting to pee outside wasn't new to me. Rex stood in front of me with his hands on his hips waiting. "I can't go with you watching!" I complained. He sighed in exasperation before turning his back to me. "You're high maintenance, lady. I've seen your lovely waxed snatch twice already, who the fuck cares if I see you piss?" I managed to lower the too-tight borrowed jeans enough down my thighs to squat and pee, Rex fidgeting the whole time impatiently.

"I need to wipe, do you have...?"

He sighed again before exhaling, "Grab a leaf, and do try to avoid one with something that bites on it."

I reached for a nearby frond of some lush palm—it did work fairly well as impromptu toilet paper.

"I'm not high maintenance. It's not easy to just let loose with someone watching." I zipped the jeans and stood. Rex turned to face me, and in one quick motion pulled open the button-fly of his canvas cargo pants. "It's a bodily function, sweetheart, it's nothing special," he barked. My eyes were glued to his crotch as he flopped out the most massive penis I'd ever seen in my life—in person, anyway. Even flaccid and wrapped in his gargantuan paw, it was still larger than life. With no regard for my gaping stare, he produced a loud, heavy stream of urine onto the verdant jungle floor. "See?" I couldn't answer—I was speechless at not only the size of his dick, but at the metal running across it—I wasn't exactly innocent, but I'd never seen a pierced penis in person. He gave his gigantic member a quick shake and shoved it back into the canvas pants. I didn't see any sign of undergarments—just King Rex and his enormous pierced cock—commando. "You're lucky we have plenty of drinkable water—if we didn't, that would have been your morning coffee, Princess," he added, pointing to the pool of urine near his feet.

"Where do we wash our hands?" I asked, palms in the air.

Ignoring me, he turned quickly and walked toward the clearing in large strides as I struggled to keep up with him. "Hurry so we can catch up. Those douche nozzles won't last long without supervision."

"I'm supposed to be your sister? Joanie?"

"Uh, yeah—*step-sister*, important distinction in case we get caught fucking."

"I'm *never* going to have sex with you!" Despite my protest, the idea of touching him caused my heart to skip a beat.

"Never say never, Princess."

"Um, no, I won't. I'm with Nate...sorta." I wasn't exactly sure what my status was with Nathaniel Slater.

"You're fucking Nate because I allowed it—he belongs to me, Penelope. You want me, sweetheart, I'm just not so sure that I'm interested yet."

I stopped walking—my feet refused to move as I absorbed his words. "You arrogant prick," I hissed at his back.

"Watch out for snakes, Princess," he shot back over his shoulder, his pace never slowing.

I stood still as the distance between us grew. No one had ever spoken to me that way—and yet, deep down I knew he was right. I wanted him more than I wanted air.

My resolve was quickly tested when an unnaturally-neon green lizard no bigger than my hand scurried across my stubborn foot. "Shit!"

Rex never looked back. "Nate would have been my knight in shining armor if he were here!" I screamed at his back before breaking into a run to catch up with him.

When I finally made it to within feet of him, he stopped and turned. Huffing and puffing, my hands fell to my thighs as I struggled for air. I was in decent shape, but between the dehydration and the lack of food, I was hurting.

He ducked down to look me straight in the eye. "You don't need a knight, Penny, or any man to save you. What you need is a good spanking—and then you need to grow the fuck up and start acting like the badass woman that you are. I have work to do, and once again, you're a monkey wrench in my life. Danger or not, I'm shipping you back to the States the second we get back to the compound—are we clear?"

I nodded, sniffling and fighting back the tears that threatened to fall. As twisted as it may sound, Rex's words were the nicest thing anyone had ever said to me. Not that I was pretty, not that I knew where the best parties were, and not that I gave good head. But, a man like him could see something badass in me. I was blown away—and I didn't want to go home.

"I-I'm sorry," I blubbered as he turned to leave me behind.

I caught up—he slowed down to cut me a little slack.

After a few more minutes of harsh silence, I could see the small band of men milling around a fallen log at the entrance to a dense section of jungle.

The younger guy, Joe, waved to Rex. "Here? Or go in further?" he shouted to Rex across the distance.

Rex silently gave the man a thumbs up gesture as we approached.

"Okay, guys, let's catch some lunch. We don't catch anything, you don't eat. In that section over there," he pointed, "spread out. You need to find trails where animals are running through these low vines. Your backpacks have snare wire—I'm going to quickly give you a demo, then it's all you. Set as many snares as you can, then grab your knife and try to stab something. Don't forget to load up on that DEET insect junk before you start. And," he warned, looking directly at me, "I want absolute silence during the hunt."

After his demonstration to the group on how to set a snare, as well as the proper way to humanely dispose of the catch, he set the group loose to hunt.

With the men off hunting, he turned his attention to me. "Well, *sis*, I don't have an extra kit for you, but I have an extra knife you can use. The snare thing is useless anyway—it would take multiple snares for days to nab enough meat to make it worth the energy expenditure. I just want them to learn various ways of obtaining food." I stood speechless as he handed me a large knife in a leather scabbard. "You're joking—I'm not going to kill anything! I can't. Rex, *please*."

"Of course you can. That rainforest," he pointed his own knife toward the overgrown jungle, "is so full of food only an idiot would starve here. Surviving off the land in Colombia is child's play. Go stab something, and because you look so hot in those snug jeans, I'll be a gentleman and show you how to clean it."

Without another word, he walked into the lush jungle and left me standing there alone—alone and freaked out.

I sat in the grass for half an hour as my stomach howled. His words rang out in my head: *"You need to grow the fuck up and start acting like the badass woman that you are."* He was right—I'd been floundering for years. My mother's long, grueling illness had leveled me. After college, I did nothing but shop during the day and cruise exclusive clubs at night collecting men. Most of them, all of them, looked like Nate. Rich, pretty, and coveted by the less-connected, less-spoiled women who, unlike me, were able to maintain a size two. A man like Rex would never be attracted to the shallow, trivial Penelope Sedgewick that lived in a Las Vegas casino penthouse. But, I knew damn well he *was* attracted to the captured Penny who was in Colombia. I liked myself here a lot more than I did at home, I decided, as I stood up and rubbed the insect repellent into my skin.

With knife in hand and head held high, I ventured into the moist jungle.

Rex was right—the place was teeming with life. Hunting would never be my thing, but I could see the value of being able to survive if I had to. My mind raced through the list of small mammals that Rex instructed the group to be on the lookout for—I mentally kicked myself for not paying better attention to his lesson.

It took me an hour to happen upon what resembled a large rat sitting in the heavy foliage under a canopy of trees. With the quietest footsteps I could manage, I crept up behind it, and in a flash stabbed it with my knife. Well, *tried* to stab it, anyway. The minute my arm lunged toward it, the tiny creature was gone. My knife sunk into the marshy earth as my body crashed into the muddy jungle floor.

Before I could think, a massive, fat snake fell from above and landed several feet in front of me. I was frozen in place, the snake and I in a catatonic stand-off. My worst nightmare sat there, its beady eyes staring into mine. A voice began to scream, to howl—a voice I recognized from my out-of-body state as my own. I screamed, and screamed, and screamed—the snake never moving.

The demon was brown with marbled markings, his pink forked tongue occasionally darting out at me like a threat. I was sure he was the devil incarnate, there to drag me to hell. The snake was bigger around than my thigh and longer than I was tall. I continued to howl, slowly trying to free myself from the quicksand-like mud I was immersed in. The villainous snake continued its evil stare.

Footsteps—I heard footsteps!

"Penny, I mean *Joanie*, very nice work. Now kill it." Rex stood nearby, the small group of men babbling to each other in nervous excitement before Rex shushed them.

"Please, Rex, please—it's going to kill me! I have a phobia—I'm terrified of snakes!"

"Nonsense. Sophocles said 'To him who is in fear, everything rustles.' That's the case here, sweetheart. Get up and kill that fucking snake—we're all hungry, and that plump bastard is a feast!"

"I *can't*." My voice was barely above a whisper.

"Fight or run, Princess. Those are your options."

I clawed my way out of the mud while they watched, Rex forbidding anyone to help me. As I stood, he walked toward me and handed me the machete they'd been using to fight their way through the jungle. I took the machete and approached the docile reptile.

"Will he bite me?" I asked calmly.

"No," Rex answered confidently. "Chop off the head."

My arm swung at the snake with every bit of power I possessed. I didn't want to miss again and be bitten. In one stroke, the head of the snake was separated from its meaty body.

"Well done," Rex praised, walking toward the snake. "Kick the head to the side." I did as I was told numbly, my fear of the snake dissipating like a vapor.

Rex pulled me into him, the clay-like mud I was covered in soiling his clothes. "See? You *are* a badass," he whispered in my ear. Suddenly my lips were on his, kissing him without thought of the group watching us. His tongue stroked against mine as someone whispered, "I thought that was his sister?"

"Step," I heard Joe answer. "Barely related," he tried to assure the shocked group.

Rex pulled back and looked at the gaping group of men. "Takes a woman to kill something worth skinning, I see. Well done, sis." He patted me on the back and reached toward the snake. "I'll cook 'er up if you'll share?" I nodded, still in shock at the last hour.

I chased after him as he carried the still moving corpse of the snake toward the clearing. The hungry men followed, and he yelled to one of them to start a fire and find a roasting stick.

"You knew I had it in me," I mused as he peeled the skin from the fatty body of the serpent. The fire was going, and Rex cleaned the snake as I sat on a log across from him.

"Well, not really. I hoped, but that boa wasn't going to hurt you, sweetheart. They bite a little, but aren't venomous. A five-foot long boa constrictor wasn't going to take you on, baby. You're too big for her to eat, and on top of it," he said as he bit his lip to pull at a particularly stubborn section of skin, "she was digesting a recent kill, that's why she wasn't moving."

"It's female?"

He nodded.

"She really is beautiful," I noticed, looking at the richness of her markings. "I feel bad now that I killed her."

"Nah, we needed the food out here. These snakes are everywhere—most common pet snake in America, in fact. She'd have probably been eaten by something else anyway—she was stuck out in the open and vulnerable. If we weren't going to eat her this afternoon, I bet something else would be. We'll honor her sacrifice with a feast."

Taken by Two

After the meal of the snake, which I admit was delicious, it took several hours to purify the water and make camp. I was amazed that Rex was able to survive only on what he carried on his back. Later that evening, when we were finally alone in his small tent, he pulled out a silver flask. "Whiskey?" he asked with a wink.

"Yes!" I giggled like a teenager.

"Not too much—you're still recovering from the dehydration." He passed me the flask. I shuddered as I took a drink, the warmth of the alcohol a comforting presence as it slid down.

"I feel guilty not sharing a sip." I nodded toward the noisy shadows still outside telling stories around the fire.

He shook his head, his face suddenly serious. "They are all addicts, Penny. Drugs, alcohol, sex— but addicts, nonetheless. Filthy rich addicts hoping to shake their demons with a high-priced, exclusive survival course taught by a decorated former…well, a former special ops guy."

"That's your business?" I asked, passing the flask back to him.

"Among other things," he answered. "What about you, Penny? What makes you so sad?"

"Sad?"

"There's a deep down darkness—regret maybe, I'm not sure. Discontent, that's all over you, but also a restlessness." He reached for the flask, and took a long sip in the darkness.

"Sad, yeah, I guess that's fair. My mother and I were close—she died a slow, painful death that I watched day by day. Everyone else in our upscale, fashionable world stepped away when she stopped being pretty, when things got bad. They wrapped it up in giving her privacy, or wanting to remember her the way she was bullshit—but it was really just weak-ass shallow fuckers not wanting to face their own mortality."

"Most people on earth are weak-ass shallow fuckers not wanting to face their own mortality, sweetheart."

"I know," I nodded. "But ever since—I've been so empty. Like none of it matters. I float through life looking for something that will move me."

He handed the flask back to me. "You're looking in the wrong place, Penny. Nothing, no one will ever fill that hole inside you. You have to find you."

I sat in the dark tent, my lips numb from the whiskey, listening to words that would change my life.

"Why did you let some guy from your past *kidnap* you, Penny?"

"Well, I didn't exactly... He drugged me!"

"Okay, but you fought very little. I mean, until yesterday you made no attempt to leave, offered very little resistance. We could be two psychopaths, and you? You decide to fuck your captor? You should have been scared shitless, but yet you just went along with it. Fear is your friend—and yet, you suppressed it. Do you always suppress your emotions like that?"

"I guess I do, yeah. I floated through being captured by some crazy guy from my past the same why I float through life. It took him really freaking me out to get me to act. I didn't want to die, but this whole time I thought someone would rescue me. They always have."

"We should have explained to you what was going on right off the bat. I guess in our desire to protect you from the ugly truth, we enabled that same lack of control that's been plaguing you."

"Killing that snake was life changing for me. I was lying in the mud, thinking, *'He'll save me,'* and then something just clicked—no one is going to save *me* but *me*."

Between the two of us, we drained the flask. As the noise of the men outside faded, we fell into each other. Rex wove his hands through my hair, pulling my face up toward his. "You surprised me today, Penny. I suspected underneath that silly façade, there was something of substance—but the snake? Never did I think you'd machete a fucking Colombian Boa!" I wrapped my arms around his powerful torso as we snuggled in closer. "There's something here—about this place, about the two of you...I feel like I just woke up from a long, dark nap. Please don't send me home, Rex. I'll behave."

He gave me a quick kiss before answering with a grin, "You won't behave. But, you've brought a lightness to our existence here. I mean with Nate, it all changed for the better. But now with you, I don't know *what* it is, but I know it's something."

His mouth ground against mine again, eager this time—needy. My hands hunted for the opening to his pants, tearing at the fabric until the head of his cock popped free from the waistband. "Do you really want me, Penny? Or are you just going along with what you think is expected?" I shook my head, sure for the first time in forever what I really wanted. At that moment, I wanted Rex. "I want you *so* badly right now," I answered. His tongue plowed into my throat, his muscular arms wrapped around my back in a strong embrace. I brushed my palm against the silky skin of his erection, the metal I'd seen earlier felt cold against my hand. I couldn't help but wonder where else his magnificent body might be tattooed or pierced.

We fell to the ground together, not taking the time to unroll the small sleeping bag. "Do you have a...?" I asked as he pulled my jeans off, his tongue diving into my soaking wetness. "*Mm,*" he groaned against my throbbing sex, "uh, no, I haven't...I've been...I don't do this. But you—God I want *you.*"

"I get the birth control shot, but *always* use protection. Well, always until Nate..."

His tongue flicked at my clit, my back arching as he sucked me into oblivion.

"I'm clean, Nate's clean—I tested him myself after his last binge," he said in a grunt, his hands wrapped around my hipbones. "Flip over, baby."

"What?" I wasn't thinking about logistics at that moment.

"You're small...tight. This...it'll be easier to take doggie style. Besides, I've been craving that damn sexy ass since the minute I saw you."

I flipped over, face down, ass up as the impossibly swollen head of his cock twitched against me. His fingers slid into me, twisting, prodding, sending me fast toward another orgasm. As I slid down from the climax, his cock was still against me, but he hadn't entered me yet. His thumb slid from my wet pussy upward, wiping the slippery fluid of my arousal toward my ass.

The sensation of pressure against my virgin asshole shocked me—with a jolt, I pulled away. "I-I've never…I can't take *that there!*" I finally choked out. "Quit thinking," he husked, "and trust me. It's just a thumb—nothing more. That's all you're ready for, all I'm prepared for in a tent in the jungle. But baby, your ass *will* be mine." His cock slid into my tight pussy, stretching me slowly until I was comfortable.

We rocked together in slow ecstasy, the perfect union of hard and soft. I spiraled again toward orgasm, his body leaned into mine, all of me opened to him. I didn't realize his thumb was inside me until it slid out, moments before his satisfied cock left me. I protested in a pout as his lips found mine once more. "Shh," he warned, "time to sleep. But you *will* belong to me, Penelope." We collapsed together, our tired bodies ignoring the dampness of the ground beneath us as we slept coiled in each other's arms.

"You shouldn't be here," I heard him say gently.

My eyes fought to open. The deep baritone voice of Rex was rumbling just outside the thin tent walls. It was early morning, and he was talking to another man, whom I could just barely hear.

"You didn't call me—she ran off alone, afraid. I was worried about her, Rex." *Nate!*

"I'm sorry, man." There was a pause. "Don't look at me like that. I sent the text saying she was safe, and you know what the fucking cell signal is like out here, but yeah, I'm sorry I didn't try harder to call. I guess I did want some time alone with her."

Their voices sank to whispers—their intimate outline visible against the canvas of the flimsy tent.

"Yeah, you were right about her. She's…special." Rex's voice finally rose loud enough for me to hear.

Nate spoke, but I couldn't make out what he was saying.

"Uh, we did, yeah…" Rex's deep voice answered.

"Holy shit, you ended a two year celibacy with Penny!" Nate's hand was on Rex's bulging shoulder. I was worried Nate would be angry, jealous—but his voice was happy and surprised.

"Shh, dude, quiet," I could just hear Rex warn Nate casually.

"I'm glad, I thought she'd help us for some reason. Maybe you can let go of the past and heal now?"

"Slow down a little, but yeah—it feels good to be out there again. Thanks to you."

They were close, huddled together outside the tent, but I couldn't see exactly *how* close.

"Okay, yeah man, take her home. You're armed, right?"

Rex spoke again, his strong arm over Nate's shoulders. "Keep our girl safe until I get back. We'll unfuck this somehow, together. I have to finish this course with these guys…yeah, Joe's back *again*. At least you're not. I'll see you and Penny in two days."

Footsteps shuffled until there was a hand on the edge of the tent. "Nate—have fun, but that luscious backside is *mine*."

Nate's rich voice answered with a comedic, "Yes, sir!"

His hand pulled back the flap to the little tent, and the tall Nate ducked to climb in, with Rex directly behind him. "Morning babycakes," he teased as my smile lit up. I didn't realize how much I'd missed him, or how attached to him I was becoming. "I'm sorry I ran, I got confused—misunderstood things. I won't—" The tears fought their way to my puffy eyes.

Nate crawled over next to me. He looked like perfection—and smelled even better. After two days in the same clothes and no bathing, Rex and I weren't exactly our freshest, and the scent of Nate's expensive, spicy cologne was heavenly. Rex sat across from us on the ground. "Penelope," he said directly to me, his thick index finger pointing inches from my face, "I need you to obey Nate. I know submission isn't your strong suit, but this is important. He may look like some GQ model, and smell like a salon in Paris, but he's tough and knows what he's doing. There are some dangerous and pissed off people here in Colombia far scarier than the ones in Vegas. Get back to our place as quickly as you can and *stay* there."

He turned to Nate.

"Make her listen. Believe me, it's not easy. If she doesn't, toss her to the snakes," he said with a grin, his wide hand reaching over to fluff up my hair.

Rex started to pack up camp as Nate and I stood to leave. Rex pulled me into his arms, his large frame leaning in to kiss me. At first I pulled back—kissing the man I was screwing in front of the *other* man I was *also* screwing was awkward. Even worse, I was developing strong feelings for both of them—for the first time I could remember, my feelings were far beyond sexual.

Rex's fingers tightened their grip on my chin. His midnight blue eyes locked onto mine—he was angry. "Pull away from my kiss like that again and it'll be the last." I nodded. *This man was intense.*

Still preoccupied by Nate watching, I wrapped my arms around Rex's muscled torso and tiptoed up to kiss him. His lips were hard on mine, forceful, possessive—I wasn't sure if the show of power was for my benefit or Nate's. His tongue explored my mouth as he pulled me closer, his fingertips digging into my ass and his bulging hardness pressing into my yielding body. "Better," he snorted when his lips finally slid from mine.

Rex's kiss left me wobbly, and it took me a second to realize that Nate was behind me, his own erect cock pressing into me. Nate's arms were around my waist as he held me close—his own lips only inches from ours. Rex didn't let go of me, but nodded toward Nate. "Nathaniel may have a kiss," he said as if giving us a gift. I twisted my face toward Nate's and, still cradled between the two strong men, my lips brushed against Nate's—his gentle, loving kiss in beautiful contrast to Rex's primal one seconds before.

I pouted as they both pulled their bodies from mine. Being sandwiched in between those two glorious men was the single most erotic experience of my life up until then, and we were all fully dressed.

"Almost home, Penny," Nate chirped as he cut through some oppressive vines blocking our path. Despite the jungle heat and the difficulty of our hike, he barely broke a sweat. "I smell so bad," I whined as he pulled me along the path. "You do smell bad," he joked, holding his nose in mockery, "but I'd tap that anyway." I smacked at him as he made some joke about hosing me down in the yard before letting me in the house.

"How much further?" I grumbled. I was exhausted, hungry, and very thirsty. "Not far, around this corner to the guard gate——"

"That's far enough, gringo."

An ominous looking man stood in front of us, his legs spread in a wide V, his hands on his hips.

Nate put his hand out to stop me from moving closer to the man.

"José, what's this about, now?" His voice was calm, almost cordial.

The man pointed a dark finger at Nate. "We have business, you owe me money."

"Ah," Nate answered, running his left hand through his hair, then casually letting it rest behind his back—where the gun stuck into his waistband. "This doesn't involve the lady—why don't we send her inside so we can chat." He gave me a quick pat on the back as if to urge me to head into the compound.

"I think I might like to keep this bitch as collateral."

"I'd be careful calling Rex's lady names, José. He can be brutal—do you remember what happened to your cousin?"

The man, José, flinched at the mention of his cousin. "I've got no problem with Rex or his girl—but we sent a *shipment* for you that you never paid for."

Nate maintained his calm demeanor, but the tension was palpable—the situation was dangerous.

"I didn't pay because I didn't accept it—I'm not doing that shit anymore. Besides, Rex has all my money; you know that. If I owe you, you have to take it up with him."

The man sighed, his mouth sinking into a grimace. "This is bullshit, and I'll be back." He turned and left, Nate's hand never leaving the loaded gun until the man was out of sight.

"Let's go get you a nice bath," he said as if nothing had happened.

"Nate, what did he mean? What was he—?"

"Let's talk in the suds, you smell like Rex's armpit right now."

"How often do you sniff Rex's armpits, loverboy?"

He laughed out loud. "Not as often as I'd like," he said pulling me inside.

Chapter Four

"What was it like?" I was leaned back against Nate's strong chest in his luxurious bathtub, his long legs wrapped around mine, as he dripped soapsuds down my chest.

"What was what like?" I asked languidly, ready to sleep.

"Being with him…touching him…making love to him?" His tone was dreamy, as if he were imagining the experience.

"Are you pissed off?" I still wasn't convinced what happened between Rex and me was okay. I felt guilty, like I'd betrayed Nate.

"Mad? No! I'm thrilled. I mean…there's no one else in the world I'd share you with, Penelope Sedgewick, but Rex? You have no idea how much you've helped him. Since his wife…" He went silent, as if he'd revealed too much.

"I overheard you outside the tent. You said he'd been celibate two years—was that because of her?"

"Yeah," he dripped more soapsuds down me, focusing on a nipple.

"Did she die?" Rex's level of intensity, the pervasive coldness about him—all of that made me sense that something dark and morbid hung over him.

"Die? No! That bitch left him for…" He went silent again.

"Why so many secrets?"

"I-I'm sorry. It's just there's been so much sadness, betrayal, ugliness. We need to make sure we can trust you, Penny. But we both agree there's something about you…you just fit with us."

"Sex with Rex was…mind-blowing. He's *intense*…but sensual, erotic. With you, there's this natural chemistry between the two of us. We just fall into each other," I said, stroking his thigh. "It's so good, but very natural, as if meant to be. With Rex…it's like a pagan ritual or something—you just feel…engrossed. And you've seen the size of his—"

"I haven't," he cut me off sharply.

I sensed I'd gone too far. "I'm sorry, I didn't mean to be crude, I…"

"Nah, you weren't, Penny. I just…I wish I could see it, I mean…I can't really put it into words."

"Are you bisexual? No reason to be embarrassed about that."

"No! I'm not bi, I'm not gay—I'm straight, always have been. I'm *very* attracted to women, *only* women," he said, dropping the sponge and cupping my breasts with both hands. "But," he said quietly, "yeah, I'm physically attracted to Rex, but it's because he's Rex—not because of any gender. It doesn't make sense."

"It doesn't have to make sense," I said with finality, turning around to snuggle into his chest. His arms wrapped around my back, pulling me close. "I knew I needed you," he whispered into my ear.

"Nate, I love being here, I feel like I'm home. But...why did you take me?"

He paused, rubbing slow circles over my shoulder blades. "I didn't tell you because I didn't want you to freak out. But—Rex was hired to kill you."

It took a minute for the meaning of his words to sink in. "What?" I finally shouted, "Rex...*me?*" I couldn't put together a coherent sentence.

"Calm down, babe. I overheard a man offer Rex a buttload of cash to abduct and eventually do away with you. Those were his words. Rex refused, and after some tension, the mysterious man left. I, of course, remembered you from years ago—I had a crush on you, but also—just felt we'd someday cross paths. Rex turned the job down, but there are plenty of others I knew would accept. I tricked Rex into going with me to Vegas—I told him I wanted to see my father—but instead I captured you."

My mind was reeling. "Rex *kills* people?"

"Not anymore," Nate answered defensively, "and certainly not *for hire.*"

"Who would want me...why?" It made no sense. I meant very little to anybody between the time my mother died and when I fell into these two men in Colombia.

"I don't know, but I knew I had to protect you. That night on the plane—Rex watched us...I knew then that you might be the connection we needed to make us complete. Rex loves me...he says I captured him, but the truth is he saved me in so many ways. We pulled each other away from destruction—together, we are so much better. But something was missing—he was never going to be able to allow the sort of relationship I craved. But you, Penny—you've awakened him. And, he's done the same for you. You are so much stronger, so different after being out in the jungle with him."

"I killed a snake!" I gloated.

He smiled wide. "I heard! You are so much more than you think you are. I'm so...I'm falling hard for you, Penelope Sedgewick." He kissed me, the bubbles crinkling between us in the cooling bathwater.

We dried off, and Nate carried me to bed in his arms. His room was elegant, expensive—his style, recreated in Rex's utilitarian compound in the middle of the rainforest. In the silky Italian sheets, he hovered over my naked body, still dewy from the long bath, and drew my face to his. "I-I'm falling for you, Pen, I can't help it." I pressed my lips to his, inhaling him, before pulling back to answer, "I've already fallen, Nathaniel."

Nate was tireless—he could come hard and unrelenting, then go again without even withdrawing from me. His desire to please me, to make me shake with pleasure, fed his own arousal. I'd never known a man like him. That night, we made love for hours until eventually we collapsed wrapped in each other, the howling of the creatures of the night lulling us to sleep.

Sometime before dawn, we stirred, our bodies joining one more time in a sleepy embrace. Afterward, the dark morning was quiet and still. "Why does Rex control your money?" I asked with a yawn.

"To protect me. I've recovered, Penny, I'm clean—thanks to Rex. But, like any addict, I've had setbacks. After the last time, I turned over control of my finances to keep from ever buying again."

"So all of this is yours?"

"No," he yawned. "The plane is, but Rex had this place before we met, and he does very well from his business."

"How much does he make killing people," I asked without thinking.

"Pen, he doesn't...I know he did some classified shit in the military and after, but that's all. People like me pay a lot of money for his guidance— don't be surprised when you get his bill for *your* time in the jungle," he said, kissing my shoulder as I drifted off to sleep.

Nate and I scurried around the next day, watching the rain pour down and anxiously awaiting the return of the larger-than-life Rex Renton. There was one text from him saying that the heavy rain was slowing them down on their journey back. Nate tried to call, but couldn't get through to Rex's Blackberry. We went to sleep that night, curled together in Nate's bed in post-coital bliss.

"Move over." The gruff whisper in my ear roused me in the wee hours of the morning. It took me a moment to process that Rex was really there, damp and smelling of soap. I slid into Nate, making room for the boxer-brief clad Rex to lie down behind me. Nate was sound asleep, barely responding when I nudged him over. I rolled toward Rex.

"You're home!"

"Uh huh," he muttered. "Tired," he said, his eyes closing as he wrapped his powerful arms around me. I fell back to sleep in the warm embrace of the two most fascinating men I'd ever known.

When I woke up, Rex was still in a deep sleep behind me, his arms and legs entwined with mine as if he were making sure I didn't leave. He'd shaven after his middle of the night shower, his skin smoother than I'd ever seen it. I planted a kiss on his cheek as Nate opened his bedroom door carrying a tray. "You made breakfast?" I whispered, trying to let Rex sleep. "Maria," he whispered as he set the tray down at the end of the wide bed. I untangled from Rex's vine-like embrace and scooted toward Nate, who handed me a cup of coffee. "He looks so innocent when he sleeps," I joked, picking at a fluffy croissant. "Sleeping lion, maybe," Nate said, munching on a sugary donut.

Rex took a deep breath and rolled over, his washboard-hard abs flexing as he exhaled. "Any other piercings besides that one," I whispered to Nate, pointing at Rex's metal-impaled right nipple, "and of course, the peen-jewelry?" Nate's eyes widened as he attacked a jelly donut.

"What? Rex Junior is *pierced*? Are you serious?"

I nodded with a giggle.

"Oh holy fuck," Nate laughed, shoving the last of the sticky donut into his mouth.

On our second cup of coffee, Rex still in deep sleep, I asked, "Has he ever slept in here before?"

Nate shook his head. "Hell no! I'm shocked…and pretty damn over the moon."

"And I never will again if you two don't shut the fuck up and let me sleep," Rex growled from underneath a pillow.

We snickered like kids, shushing each other as we packed up our breakfast in bed.

It was noon before Rex finally emerged from Nate's bed. He stumbled into the kitchen, still in his underwear, ran a hand through his sexy bedhead, and told Maria to make him steak and eggs. As he sat at the breakfast bar reading a newspaper in Spanish, I spied on him from around the corner. "Come in, Penny," he eventually said like an exasperated parent.

I came out of hiding from the doorframe and slinked up to sit on a stool next to him. "Why are you hovering?" he asked patiently as Maria placed his plate in front of him. "I missed you, that's all. You were asleep forever."

"I've been in the jungle for a week, Princess. And, I'm nearly twice your age. I needed a little sleep. Where's Nate?" He glanced back at his newspaper.

"He said he needed to go into the city to buy supplies. He'll be back this afternoon."

"He go alone?" Rex flipped a page in his paper.

"No, he went with one of the drivers."

Rex nodded, not looking up, before shoveling eggs into his mouth.

When he'd finished eating, he folded his paper and leaned back with a mug of black coffee. I was nervous, unsure of what to do next, and felt out of place in his house. "Okay, Penny, you're not a prisoner here," he said with a sigh. "I feel it's dangerous for you to leave, and I'd like you to stay with us until it's safe for you to go back. Can you do that?" He looked pointedly at me. "Yes," I answered heartily. "Good then," he smiled, "let's get to know each other." I sat across from him, waiting. "When did you get your last birth control shot? Was it Depo-Provera?" he asked gruffly. "I-uh, I'm not sure…" I felt like I was sitting in the gynecologist's office all of a sudden. "Do you need to look at a calendar?" he snapped. "No, uh, it was…May fifth." He nodded, satisfied that I wouldn't need another dose anytime soon. "Your turn, what do you want to know?" I smiled, surprised he was willing to open up with me. "Uh, okay, who hired you to kill me?" His expression never changed, but he slid his plate toward Maria and said, "No comment. Discussion over."

"I'm sorry," I apologized as I followed him from the kitchen.

"It's fine," he shot back. "I have work to do. You can move into that room," he pointed across a long hallway, "where you'll be more comfortable."

"I liked us all together," I argued, still chasing after him as he turned a corner and headed into a room. "Penny, we'll see on that, okay? I don't really want to talk about it right now."

Rex closed the door and didn't come back, and Maria pretended not to speak much English when I tried to ask questions about the compound. I walked back to the room where I'd stayed before escaping into the jungle. It wasn't locked anymore. I packed the borrowed things and the toiletries from the small bathroom and wandered back into the main house and down a long hallway to the room Rex indicated I was to use. The room was elegant, and the same richness that decorated Nate's room flowed through this one, but this room was feminine. The four-poster bed was covered in sheer canopy draping, and the bed was stacked high with plush silk throw pillows. I set down the duffle bag of clothing, and turned a corner toward a spacious marble bathroom. A vanity table sat in the corner, a velvet bench sat elegantly in front of it. *A woman lived here...* To my disappointment, there was no makeup in the bathroom—I missed my eyeliner. On the side of the bathroom, an enormous walk-in closet sat empty. A few hangers hung on the wood rails, but other than that it was stripped bare.

Back in the main bedroom, I flopped onto the bed. There were a few paperbacks in the nightstand, but little else. Bored and lonely, I flipped on the flatscreen television mounted to the wall. Unlike the TV in the locked room, this one had full satellite hooked up. As I flipped channels, most in Spanish, I eventually found several American channels and fell asleep watching one of them.

I woke from my nap in Nate's arms, some soccer game on TV. "Sleeping beauty," he teased, a lopsided grin crossing his lips. "I hate it here without you—I feel unwelcome," I whined. He pulled me tighter and kissed my forehead. "You're very welcome, it's just we're not used to having guests here, and certainly not a woman. Rex wants you to stay—he told me we're having dinner out by the pool tonight—the three of us. I've never known him to plan anything like a meal with others before. You're good for him, Penny."

I curled up in Nate's embrace, inhaling the rich scent of his spicy cologne. "Who's room was this?" I asked, my lips at his neck. "It was Evelyn's room, his wife." I looked around—I couldn't imagine Rex in here. "They had separate rooms?" Nate ran his fingers through my hair. "I don't think so—I think he set it up to please her. She wasn't happy to be brought to Colombia."

"Why did *you* come here? To Colombia?"

"Oh, to take Rex's survival course."

"So that's how you got clean, by spending a week in the jungle?"

He shook his head, a look of regret falling like a curtain. "No, I left the second night—ended up in Medellin and…" He trailed off and never finished, the sadness washing over him. I kissed the soft skin of his collarbone, my kisses trailing up his neck until my lips crashed onto his, his lips opening as my tongue slid in. The bulge of his erection in his fitted jeans drew my hand to it, stroking up and down as it grew. "Nate," I moaned. "Penny, stop…" His hand covered mine, pulling it away from his hardness.

"Why?" I was confused. "Is everything okay between us?"

He smiled and stroked my cheek. "Everything is perfect. I'm so...I'm insane about you, babe. But Rex said no sex, kisses and cuddles only."

I sighed, annoyed at the control Rex wielded. "He won't know—we don't have to do what he says!" I moved to stroke him again, but his grasp on my wrist stopped me.

"Rex knows *everything* that happens around here. And...it's not that I *have* to obey him, it's that I *want* to obey him."

He kissed me again before sitting up. "Dinner is at seven. We're getting dressed up."

"Dressed up? I was given a few pairs of jeans, shirts, flats—I have no idea where the dress I had on went to."

"I'm sure he'll take care of it. I need to go return a few emails and get ready. Don't worry! You have two men who are obsessed with you." He winked at me before climbing out of bed and leaving my room.

Nate was such a comforting presence to me; I felt a sense of loss every time he left my side. *Dinner...* My stomach rumbled—I hadn't eaten since the pastries Nate brought to bed that morning. When I was a captive here, my meals were brought to me on a tray. Now, I really wasn't sure what my place in the house was. Rex said I was a guest, but I didn't feel like a guest. I felt like the new kid on the block at a place I never wanted to leave.

The clock by the bed said it was a quarter to six. I took a long shower, shaving everywhere I hoped would later be licked, in the gorgeous shower. *He did all this for her...* I couldn't help but be jealous that Rex loved someone—I already knew deep inside I only wanted him to love me. *Me, and Nate*, I thought. Nate said she left two years ago—but Rex still wore a heavy gold wedding band on his left ring finger. *Evelyn*...her name was immersed in the sea of ink on his tanned skin. Another name floated next to it, Noah. The name Noah was intertwined with a rose, the Virgin Mary overlooking it. During our time together, I wanted to ask Rex about his tattoos—they clearly were meaningful to him, and not decoration—but got the feeling Rex didn't much like to be asked personal questions.

When I emerged from the long, steamy shower, I noticed a bathrobe hanging on a hook near the door. I didn't remember it being there before. I dried off with one of the fluffy white towels, and wrapped my long hair in another. The robe was warm as I slipped it on. Maria must have come in while I was showering and I didn't even notice it, I assumed.

Wrapped in the cozy robe, I walked out to the bedroom to figure out what to wear and saw a dress bag draped across the bed. The faint smell of cologne lingered—one that wasn't Nate's signature scent. This one was...earthy, clean, and very masculine. *Rex?* I wondered. I shook my head—I couldn't imagine Rex splashing on cologne. I thought the bag would contain the tiny red dress I wore the night Nate drugged me, but as I pulled the zipper down, I gasped. A delicate ivory silk gown was inside—the tiniest spaghetti straps clinging to the satin hanger. The gown was exquisite—far softer and more feminine than anything I'd normally go for. Satin pumps rested at the bottom of the bag—everything was my size. *This had to be Nate!*

I dried my hair and put the gown on—it felt like a dream against my skin. My only regret was I didn't have any makeup to apply. Nate took me from *The Penelope* without even a purse—I rarely bring much down to the club since I live upstairs and don't pay for anything in the hotel. *Just a little eyeliner would make all the difference*, I thought as I cringed in the mirror before walking from the room.

Nate was standing in the hallway outside, his dark suit shining as his face lit up when he saw me. "Penny, you look...you just took my breath away." He dipped down to kiss me, his tall frame bending to wrap around me. "Wow, just wow," he whispered as our lips parted. "You're so eloquent tonight," I teased. His eyes roamed over me before settling on mine, his expression serious. "I'm speechless, yes, but Penny, I'm falling in love with you." My heart pounded, my palms went sweaty. I felt the same for him, but I couldn't stop thinking about Rex. I never believed you could truly be in love with more than one person, but now I wasn't so sure.

Nate took my arm and started us walking. "Can't be late for King Rex, babe, he doesn't do late." He walked me to a wall of glass at the back of the house and outside. The night was warm and sticky—the raw sounds of the jungle all around. We went down a short pathway lined with lighted palm trees. We turned a corner and my eyes drank in a large infinity pool, lit from underneath, with flowers floating across the smooth surface of the water. In the corner, a cabana was lit with candles, and the vision of Rex standing from a chair surprised me. I almost didn't recognize him—he was in a suit. Not a shiny designer suit like Nate wore, but a simple dark suit that strained to fit around his muscled body.

"It fit," he said gruffly, pointing at the dress as he approached. "*You* left the dress?" He nodded, reaching for me and pulling me toward him. "Yeah, and I don't fucking shop much, so…I did my best. I've wanted to see you in something fluid—your curves deserve to be set free, worshipped—not contained in a too-tight dress."

I leaned in to give him a kiss on the freshly-shaven cheek he offered. The scent…it was the same as the cologne smell in my room. "I wish I had some makeup," I pouted, rubbing at my eyes. "Cover up that divine skin? Penelope, there's no cosmetic that could improve the perfection of your beauty tonight."

Soft Rex always threw me off balance, and I never knew how long it would last. "Thank you," I said quietly as the two men led me to a table covered in tall candles and fragrant tropical flowers. Nate pulled out my chair as Rex pulled a bottle of Champagne from a silver ice bucket. With little flourish, he popped the cork and poured the bubbling contents into three crystal flutes. He handed us each a glass, my eyes darting to Nate. "Alcohol isn't his drug of choice, Penny. Life would be easier if it were," Rex answered in response to my unspoken question. "Amen to that," Nate chuckled. "Okay, here's my goddamn toast. To whatever the mother fuck this thing is," Rex raised his glass as we did the same, clinking them together.

Rex quickly abandoned the bubbly for bourbon, with Nate and I splitting two bottles of wine as we ate. I wasn't sure if the house staff made the meal, or if it had been catered in, but the food was as good as the best starred restaurant in Vegas—and I dined at them far too frequently to be good for my figure. By the time we made it to dessert, a warm crème brulee served by Maria, Rex's hand searched my inner thigh, snaking its way up to my skimpy panties as I struggled to focus on finishing dessert. As I slid my dish back, Nate's long fingers skimmed my other thigh.

Rex's hand slid down to my knee before leaving my skin wanting his touch. He stood up and slid off his suit jacket, carefully placing it over his chair. "Do you swim, Penny?" I nodded, unable to speak as he removed his cufflinks and placed them on the table. "Good exercise, and an important survival skill," he said as he pulled his black tie loose. "I've never understood the purpose of a tie," he sighed, wrapping it around his thick wrist. I peeled my eyes from him to look at Nate—who sat rapt, his full attention on Rex.

"Maria," he gestured toward the darkness, the maid scurrying from some unseen staging area. "We're finished. Can you make sure we're not disturbed? Take tomorrow off—dinner was delicious." She nodded and answered, "Thank you, Mr. Renton," in perfect English.

When she'd cleared the remaining dishes and left the pool area, Rex unbuttoned his shirt, letting it fall to the ground. The sight of his bare skin glowing in the candlelight, the strong muscles of his chest emerging from the formal clothes, was so erotic my thighs clenched in response. He ran a hand through his hair, as if to loosen it from the restrictive hair product he'd swiped through it. "Sorry guys, I don't normally do dates and shit. I'm so far out of my comfort zone—but, I wanted to step into your world for a few hours, make an effort." He glanced down at his crisp leather shoes, reaching down to slip out of them. He continued, "But I'm going for a swim."

Pulling his long leather belt off, he momentarily wrapped it around his hands before dropping it to the ground. We were speechless, our eyes fixated on his powerful body frame. Nate gulped audibly as Rex yanked at the button of his pants, letting them fall. There was nothing underneath—just Rex's inked skin, and his heavy cock emerging as it was let loose from the confining fabric. I wanted to watch Nate, to gauge his reaction to Rex's nakedness, but my own lusty eyes wouldn't budge. I drank him in, the metal piercings reflecting in the candlelight. "Join me if you want," he offered as he turned to walk toward the deep end of the pool, his firm muscled ass a work of art as he moved.

He dove in, his sculpted body crossing the length of the pool in fluid lines. "He's beautiful," Nate finally managed to sputter, his hand seeking my skin.

"Yes," I nodded. "You *both* are."

He leaned in to kiss me, the warmth of his lips radiating through me. My fingers sought out his swollen cock, straining against the satiny suit pants. "*God, Penny, I want you so much,*" he husked.

"Come swim, you goddamn lovebirds. I didn't say you could kiss," Rex's sharp voice barked at us from across the pool deck.

Nate immediately stood, pulling me to my feet.

"We're coming," Nate answered, his eyes never leaving mine. His fingers reached up to hook through the narrow straps of my silk gown, pulling them over my shoulders and down by body until the dress sat in a pool of fabric at my feet. With his hands in mine, he guided me out of the heels and walked me toward the pool in only the skimpy silk panties.

Rex was still swimming laps, the toned muscles of his body pushing effortlessly through the water. Nate walked me to the edge, holding my hand as I sat on the rim of the pool, my feet dangling in the warm, salty water. Despite the driving lust that racked him, Nate backed up into the shadows and leaned against a palm tree, fully dressed in contrast to our nakedness. He would follow Rex's instruction, even if it left him frustrated and excluded.

He's going to fuck me in front of Nate, just to make him suffer, I thought with a mixture of excitement and dread. After several long moments, Rex ducked underwater and swam the length of the pool, emerging between my legs. "I crave you like a drug, Princess," Rex nearly moaned, pulling off the thin panties. His hands parted my thighs as his face sunk into me in animalistic need. My hands fisted at his wet hair, desperate for more contact as his agile tongue poked at my pussy.

His mouth continued to work me as I leaned back, pressing into him, begging for more as he teased me. On the brink of climax, he withdrew his tongue from me, his arms wrapping around my waist. "Please don't stop," I begged. "Patience," he scolded, his tongue darting around his lips, slick with my arousal.

He pulled me into the water with him, turning me around to face Nate as his hard cock pressed against me in the warm water. Nate's expression was obscured by the darkness, but his hand rested on the bulge of the erection straining against his pants. Rex motioned to Nate as he sunk into me, his thick cock impaling me in one motion. The intense shock of having him so deep, so suddenly, shook me, my body grasping against his as I strained to focus on Nate, who was walking toward us.

With my hands braced on the side of the pool, Rex withdrew and slammed into me again, driving my limp body against the tile wall. Rex said something to Nate, but I was too far gone from his continued slow, driving thrusts to focus on what they were talking about. Nate answered, then started to undress—the falling away of his crisp linen shirt revealing his perfect six-pack abs, the deep V of his toned torso tantalizing me like eye candy.

Nate's luscious naked body walked toward us, Rex still relentlessly fucking me from behind as his head rested on my shoulder. "Sit on the edge in front of her," he grunted to Nate. Rex's powerful body pressed me forward, toward Nate's long cock hovering larger than life in front of me. My mouth watered, I wanted to touch him but knew I was expected to wait for Rex's instruction.

"Suck him," was all Rex said, low and gravelly, as he wrapped his fist around the mass of hair at the base of my neck, shoving my willing mouth onto Nate's swollen cock. I gagged as Rex pressed me farther, Nate's hardness scraping the back of my throat and beyond. "Swallow," he grunted, his pace never relented as he fucked me to oblivion. His left hand found my clit, stroking it as he fucked me from behind. Nate moaned as I sucked him, his hands buried in the back of my head as our rhythm increased—the three of us immersed in a symbiotic union of ecstasy as we climaxed together.

Rex withdrew from me, swimming another long underwater lap as Nate held me at the side of the pool, his salty essence still on my tongue, my lips swollen from the intensity of the blowjob. Rex emerged from the pool, his golden body glistening in the sparkling ambient light. From a small pool cabana, he pulled out a stack of fluffy towels and brought them to where Nate and I were sitting. My legs were rubbery, my body weak from the ferocity of taking them both. Nate's strong arms pulled me from the water as Rex wrapped me in the oversized towel. Nate supported my weight as Rex leaned in to kiss me. "Are you okay, baby?" Rex asked softly. "I'm amazing," I answered, wobbly and drunk on the rush of pleasure. He looked over to Nate, his hand resting on Nate's shoulder. "I'm going to carry her to your room, grab the door, man," Rex instructed.

Curled up in Rex's strong embrace, I dozed off as he carried me through the house and laid me down on Nate's sumptuous bed. I came to as Rex dried me off with the towel. Nate was next to me, his naked body reclined like a Greek god across the fluffy down comforter. Both men were gloriously erect as I rolled to rest my head across Nate's legs. "More, Princess, or are you tired?" Rex's deep voice asked in my ear. "More," I begged.

I lay in Nate's lap, his hands caressing me, as Rex climbed behind me and entered me again, this time slowly, controlled. "You like watching me fuck her?" Rex asked, his grip in my hair tightening. "Yes," Nate said with a growl.

"I want her on her back," Rex instructed suddenly.

I was rolled over, my head on the downy pillows, as Rex moved between my legs, his punishing cock penetrating my sore pussy missionary-style. He kissed me, his mouth urgent, thrusting with both his tongue and cock, unable to control his carnal need for me. Nate lay next to me, watching, his cock twitching and his eyes glazed over by his excruciating lust.

In a shuddering climax, Rex spilled into me for the second time that night, his heavy body collapsing on me as my fingers clawed into his strapping back. With a final deep breath, he withdrew from me, his spent body collapsing at my side. "Clean her up," Rex barked at Nate. Pausing for a minute as Rex's words sunk in, Nate's eyes focused on my tortured pussy. "Slowly," Rex added as Nate positioned his mouth at my entrance.

Nate's delicate tongue started at my sensitive clit, teasing it while I thrashed. Rex's face was at my shoulder, his lips on my skin as he watched Nate lick my swollen folds before dipping down to drink Rex's seed from my quivering sex. I felt Rex inhale deeply as he watched his come leave my pussy to be savored by Nate's worshipping tongue.

Nate licked until there was no further trace of Rex inside me, despite my desperate pleas for him to allow me to come. Rex held me tight, his lips continuing to kiss me as he watched Nate pleasure me. As I begged for him to let me climax, Nate raised his lips to suck my clit, a finger stroking my G-spot as I writhed between the two men, the orgasm ripping through me with a vengeance.

"Yes, you may," I heard Rex answer to Nate as I descended from the brink of ecstasy.

Softly, slowly, Nate's rock-hard cock entered me—fucking me slowly, then with force as Rex held me still, driving me to yet another orgasm so intense I thought I'd explode. "*I can't...*" I moaned, "*I can't take any more.*" Nate's strong hands grasped my ribcage as he pounded me, his face twisted in painful tension as he let go, coming inside me before collapsing next to me.

We slept there, the two men at my sides, in exhausted perfection. Deep in the night, I rolled over to Rex. In the dim light I traced a finger over his shoulder, tracing the script of a name buried in the detail of a rose. "His name was Noah," he said as my fingers glided across his skin.

"Was?"

"He was my son."

The silence hung between us as I absorbed his words. Rex was wrapped in a hard, thick shell, and I knew care was needed to not push too far.

"Did he live here with you?" I asked.

"No, he never lived here. I brought Evelyn here after he died; I hoped it would help. I-I tried to save her, but of course, couldn't. Her grief took over; she left for another life."

My fingers traced the other name inked into his skin: *Evelyn.*

"I'm sorry," was all I could manage to say.

"It was my fault—all of it. We married young—she was my high school sweetheart. Evelyn worked her ass off putting me through college, then medical school. I joined the military when they offered to pay off my hefty student loans. Life was good—except Evelyn craved a baby. More than anything, she wanted to be a mother—she wanted to have someone need her. Years passed and she didn't get pregnant. I became more and more involved in search and rescue and combat medicine, and then more classified stuff with special ops task forces. The thrill of that life consumed me—I deployed more and more, and was home less and less."

"You worked here, in Colombia?"

"I can't talk about the things I did in the service, but I'll just say I fell in love with it here. The climate, the people—I never wanted to leave."

"And your wife?"

"She withered alone—she wasn't that strong."

"Did she cheat on you?"

"Never. She was loyal, she held on to me for years. But, five years ago she decided she'd had enough and filed for divorce. I went home, begged her to give me more time. I promised her that my military career was almost over. She agreed, deluding herself into thinking I would just leave the colorful life I led in the jungle to go home and set up a medical practice. Penny, I loved her, but I was *never* going to be that kind of guy."

I ran my index finger along his skin, tracing the delicate petals of the rose surrounding her name. "So you stayed together?"

"She agreed to wait on the divorce. And, on that trip home somehow, some way, we conceived a baby. But I didn't change—when Noah was born I was in the middle of the jungle, stitching up a Delta Force guy who'd been nearly gutted by a cartel thug."

I pulled into him, Nate still sleeping soundly at my back. "I just can't imagine you as a father, that's—"

"I wasn't a father. The baby died shortly after delivery—the cord was wrapped around his throat. I never even saw him in person, only in photos."

He went silent after that, rolling into me and closing his eyes. Sharing wasn't easy for this stoic man, and I knew it was time to let him go silent.

Chapter Five

The next morning, I woke up to find both men gone. I rolled over in Nate's comfy bed—the bedside clock informing me in bright blue numbers that it was after ten. I felt very naked, sore, and in need of a shower. A cozy robe was draped across the end of the bed, left for me probably by Nate. I slid it on and walked across the hall to my room. Suddenly, it felt like *her* room rather than mine. I knew if I stayed, I'd want that room redone.

I took a long, hot shower before going into the walk-in closet to throw on one of the few outfits left for me by the absent Evelyn. I was now sure these were her clothes, and probably not her A-list outfits. But...the closet was no longer empty. It was full— there were shoes, dresses, jeans, and blouses—all my size. I pulled open a drawer—panties and bras in exquisite lace and silk. Another drawer held swimsuits, and another was stocked with pajamas, some sexy, some comfy. Tears swelled in my eyes— someone cared for me. It wasn't the things that touched me, back in Vegas I had more material things than I could ever appreciate, but the fact that I was not only being cared for but being encouraged to stay touched me deeply.

I dressed, savoring the chance to look good again and put together an outfit. Back in the bathroom, I prayed they'd thought to provide me some makeup, but the vanity drawers were still empty.

When I felt presentable, I wandered down the hall in search of company. An open door off the main living space revealed Nate in a modern black leather and chrome office, staring intently at several large screens in front of him as he tapped away at a keyboard. He was dressed casually, in slim jeans and a striped oxford shirt. "Hey, lover lover," he said as he noticed me standing in front of him. "You have an office here?" I asked.

"Yeah—despite my disappearance, I still run my little empire through a few trusted contacts at my company. They're willing to let me stay hidden a little longer."

Nate's "little empire" was worth billions, and I grinned at his modesty.

I walked around his desk to crawl into his lap. He nuzzled into my hair as I looked at his screen—it was all computer code, financial graphs, and other math-looking stuff that bored me to tears. "Thanks for the clothes," I said, running my fingers through his wavy copper hair. "It wasn't just me—Rex agreed that we needed to make you feel at home. He said the clothes he gave you in the duffle bag were the few things she didn't take—I guess she forgot to check the dryer when she wiped him out. I did do the shopping, though."

"Next time you shop, can I have some makeup?"

"Uh, I thought about that, Rex likes your skin natural, though."

I sighed in exasperation. "At least some eyeliner?"

"Go ask him. I think he's in his office working." I couldn't picture Rex with an office, doing work that didn't involve a machete. "Okay, but can we go for a swim after? Maybe you can take me into town?"

"Sorry, Pen," he apologized, "I've got one of my main guys here needing my help on this—I have to put out some fires before I can go back to my life of leisure and kinky sex." He winked at me before turning his eyes back to one of his monitors. I walked to the door. "Where's his office?" He tapped on his keyboard a moment before absently answering, "Oh, directly across, on the other side of the living room."

"Am I allowed to go in there?" I still didn't understand Rex's boundaries.

"Uh, sure, yeah—nothing secret about his office." He didn't look up. "We'll hang out later, babe, I promise."

I left Nate's office, gently closing his door before walking across the expansive main living area to a closed door on the other side. I knocked softly, almost changing my mind about bothering Rex. I never knew if I'd find hard Rex or soft Rex.

"Come in," his deep voice boomed from the other side.

I pushed it open and stood at the entrance. Rex's office was the opposite of Nate's modern, sophisticated space. A worn leather bomber sofa sat in the corner, and the far wall was lined with shelving containing survival and camping gear—backpacks, knives, tents, fishing lines, and all of the other stuff he probably provided his clients. The room felt like Colombia—deep chocolate hues, lush greens, and a general feeling of chaos. It was the sort of place where you expected to see Ernest Hemingway sitting in a corner, typing and smoking a cigar. "Am I bothering you?" I asked sheepishly, hoping for soft Rex.

"No, I'm struggling with the less-fun aspect of my job." He gestured for me to come as I slinked closer. With his dark gaze on me, I suddenly felt ridiculous bothering him for something as superficial as makeup. Rex wore his standard outfit of worn jeans, black combat boots, and a black t-shirt that strained to cover his muscular frame. I couldn't take my eyes off his face, however. He was wearing glasses. "You look so scholarly!" I burst out with my usual lack of a verbal filter. He whipped them off and tossed them on the desk. "What the fuck ever, Penelope. Wait until you hit your forties."

I covered my snicker with my hand. "Come here," he said, patting his lap. "I need a distraction."

I sat down on his lap, his arms around me from behind as he stared at the screen. "Thanks for the clothes." He kissed my shoulder and clicked at something with his mouse. "You're welcome, Princess. You look beautiful, and smell even better." I smiled, my eyes looking around the room. The walls had several military plaques, different awards from different squadrons, and a framed certificate. I squinted to read it: *LT COL Roger N. Renton*. "Is that your father, Roger Renton?" I asked.

He sipped at his coffee before resting his hand on my thigh.

"Such a curious girl." He offered no answer, and went back to clicking his monitor.

"Rex, I was wondering if I could have some makeup? Maybe just some eyeliner?"

He ignored my question, rubbing his chin in confusion at the dilemma on his screen.

"You are flawless, Penny. Why the fuck would you want to alter that?"

I stroked his forearm, the intricate swirls of ink wrapping around his bulging muscles. "I-I'm glad you like the way I look. But, I'd just feel more confident with a little liner…"

He squinted at his screen—the display making perfect sense to me, unlike Nate's work. Rex needed his glasses, but didn't want to put them back on after I'd teased him. Even King Rex seemed to have insecurities.

"Uh, yeah, I guess…I want you to be happy, sweetheart. We'll pick you up some next time one of us goes into town."

My eyes focused on the travel arrangements on the screen. "You know, if you brought that guy from Omaha in on the earlier flight, you'd save $500. They arrive at about the same time in Bogotá."

He squinted at the screen before reaching for his black-framed glasses. "Well, I guess… It's only $500 though, and this guy is a big real estate mogul. I don't want to piss him off—well, until he gets out in the jungle. *Then* I'll piss him off royally." An evil grin slid across his lips. He looked from the screen to me. "This stuff makes sense to you?"

"Perfect sense. Hospitality, travel, dealing with high-rollers—I've seen it my whole life. I was born and raised in a casino, for fuck's sake."

"Such language," he slapped at my thigh. Rex used fuck in every form, at least in every third sentence—but apparently he didn't like it when I did.

"Rex, every little bit adds up. If you can save $500 without sacrificing quality, always do it. These rich folks have airport clubs they hang out in anyway—he'll get his last alcohol fix before you scare him straight," I winked.

"I see your point. I hate this shit—I just want to be in the field. I tried having one of the staff do it, but I'm worried about confidentiality, and their English isn't the best. And, Mr. Omaha isn't an alcoholic—he's addicted to Oxy after a back injury. You repeat *any* of this, I'll—"

"Throw me to the snakes?"

"Deny you sex, you horny little thing. Now, show me what would you do about this guy from Toronto—the time difference is brutal."

I took the mouse over, clicking until I had his future student from Toronto arriving closely enough to the rest of his class members to transport them to base camp together in one van. "You, Penelope Sedgewick, are smart as fuck." He gave me a quick squeeze from behind.

"My dad would never let me help with any of the business—he said I was an airhead and would never get it, said to go back to shopping and drinking for a living."

"He's an idiot," Rex pronounced with finality, "for more reasons than that, believe me."

"I'm so bored...can I help with your business?"

"Hm," he murmured. "You'd be a great help, sweetheart. Help me finish this, and we can play."

I finished the routing, then looked at his ground transportation network, as well as his departure lounge set-up before he reached up and clicked the screen off. "Turn around," he commanded. I clamored around to straddle him, looking into his eyes. He was silent, his arms wrapping around my waist.

"I loved the date last night," I said to break the silence.

"It was out of my comfort zone, but I mostly did it for Nate."

"For *Nate*?" I asked, the tinge of jealousy rising in me.

He nodded, his fingertips brushing across my face to pull my lips out of their childish pout.

"I wanted to show Nate that we were three— not you and I, and sure as fuck not you and him. It's just been the two of us for so long, not in a sexual way, but we've been close. I guess our...it's more than a friendship, more than brotherly, but not... I can't explain it, but I knew he wanted more, I just couldn't provide it. But with you here...it's like a missing piece clicked into place last night."

"Do you mean through me, you can let Nate get close to you in a more physical way?"

"I'm not sure—maybe, at least to some degree. Last night was much more than sex...it was..."

"Spiritual," I whispered.

He nodded and went silent.

"This is all new to me, and so fucking far out of what I know—but I *do* know that Nate helped pull me back to life, and without him, I'd be dead. I'm willing to try to give him some of what he needs, at least as much as I can without losing my own boundaries. And you, Penny, are making me feel happiness for the first time in years." He pulled me close, my head resting on his hard chest. "Will you stop being so bossy?" I prodded, pushing my luck.

"Never. I can't function without control—too much shit has happened to me that's been beyond my control. I only feel safe if I'm in charge. Nate gets that—he doesn't obey because he's weak or even submissive. Nate is a strong, testosterone filled bulldog of a man, but he realized early on that to have any type of relationship with me, he had to let me lead. And he did...until he tricked me into going with him to Las Vegas to rescue a blonde in danger that he'd never forgotten." His lips brushed the top of my head as he held me.

"Am I in danger still?"

"Yes, baby, you are. We *all* are. The second word gets out that you're here, and it will eventually get out, it'll be war. Not only did I turn down the offer to kill you, but I turned around and prevented the guy who was hired from doing the job. Shit will hit the fan, sweetheart."

I rose up to look at him, afraid and stricken with the reminder that this wasn't a vacation. My life was in danger. *Who would hire someone to kill me? And why?*

These two men had become my everything in such a short time, I couldn't let them be harmed. "I'll go back—my father will protect me. I don't want you two to be—"

He jerked my face to his, his jaw clenched. "I want you to be mine, to be *ours*. Don't ever talk about leaving here for us—*we* will fucking protect you, not that…" He bit his lip to keep from continuing with his feelings for my father—whom he seemed to know, or at least know about.

"Do you want to be with us?" His voice was calm, serious.

I nodded, a tear meandering down my cheek. He wiped it away with a fingertip. "We'll keep you safe, Penny. We…" He paused, as if once again suppressing the words he longed to say. "We care about you. You belong here with us."

After a long silence, my eyes fell again to the many plaques on the wall.

"Who's Roger?" I asked, desperate to be let in to his shrouded world.

"Me."

"Oh! I though maybe he was your father. You don't seem old enough to be a Colonel—"

"*Lieutenant* Colonel—that's the rank I left the military at. My *father* was a dead-beat heroin junkie sperm donor who beat the living shit out of me every chance he had. He never amounted to anything."

I brushed my lips across his scratchy neck—falling more in love with him every time he shared himself with me. He leaned in to touch his nose against my forehead. "Rex is a nickname the para-rescue guys gave me in honor of my innate jungle skills—Rex, King of the Jungle—I guess it stuck."

He gave me a playful swat on the ass and said, "Okay, Princess, climb off. I promised we'd play—and I *desperately* need some play."

"Um, should we get Nate?" I licked my lips and salivated at the thought of sex with both of them together again.

"No, he doesn't play."

"What?" I asked, my face scrunched in a question. The kind of play I wanted to do was very much something Nate did—did very well, in fact.

"I mean, he can shoot, but he doesn't really like to just go out and blast things."

It dawned on me that Rex wasn't talking about sex. "Guns? I-I've never shot a gun!"

"Oh baby, let me pop your cherry then." He stood up and walked over to a heavy wool rug on the floor in the corner. He pulled it up, revealing the solid wood floor underneath. He pushed at one of the planks before pulling up a metal door. Below the door were a half dozen military-looking rifles next to as many handguns. "That's your arsenal?" I asked, surprised. "Arsenal? Hell, that's just my safe here *in this part of the house*. It is one of many, sweetheart, one of *many*. Tools of the trade, baby."

We walked out of the compound, Rex loaded down with guns, ammunition, and other shooting equipment, until we came to a clearing where he had various targets and objects to shoot at set up. I was a little nervous, my only exposure to firearms was the many security people that were around my dad's businesses, but I'd never held or shot any myself. "What if—what if the gun just goes off?"

"That's what we're here for today, Penny. Guns don't just go off by themselves, baby," he stuck up his index finger in front of him and curled it as if pulling the trigger on the gun. "It doesn't do anything until *you* make it—you pull the fucking trigger, it fires. Once you know what you're doing, guns are only dangerous to the people that you point them at, which is why you're going to learn."

Rex pulled out a handgun, examined it for a second, and then handed it to me grip first. The grip of the pistol felt like rough sandpaper. It smelled like a combination of oil and charcoal. It was a lot heavier than I expected, and partly made of plastic and partly made of metal.

He handed me safety glasses and I put them on, thinking that they were extremely ugly. "Okay, this line," he traced a line etched in the dirt with the toe of his heavy boot, "is the firing line. You don't go past it unless I tell you to. Point your weapon that way," he pointed toward the targets. "Not at me, not at your feet, not at the compound—only that way. Always assume that every gun you touch is loaded, and assume that if you pull the trigger, it's going to shoot. This," he showed me a lever on the pistol, "is the safety. This way, the safety is on and you can't pull the trigger," Rex flicked the lever with his thumb, "and this way, the safety is off; when you pull the trigger, it will shoot. This gun has fifteen rounds—it's a semi-automatic, so you don't have to cock it each time."

"You said cock," I joked.

He shot me the knock-it-off look, and continued. "The slide is spring loaded. You rack it like this…" He grasped the top of the slide of his own pistol, pulled it back, and let it loose. The metal slide slammed shut with a loud metallic snap. "That loads the first cartridge in the chamber."

"This gun isn't very powerful, so there won't be much recoil, but keep a firm grip on the weapon after it fires, like this…" His hands braced the gun in demonstration.

"I'm bored," I whined, his stern glare silencing me. "You *will* learn this shit, Penny. This is serious. It could save your life…or mine."

"Yes, sir," I sighed.

"I want you to load your first cartridge the way I showed you."

I racked the gun, satisfied that I did it the way he'd demonstrated.

Rex stood behind me, his massive arms outside of mine, showing me how to grip the handgun. "Hold it just like this in your dominant hand, a firm grip, just like a handshake. Grasp with your support hand—your left hand—around the outside of your right. Wrap it around to completely support the grip of your other hand."

"Okay stand like this…legs a shoulder-width apart, knees loose, keep your back straight…Yeah, like that, perfect. Shows off that delicious ass, too. I'm gonna break that virgin ass in very soon, Princess."

I couldn't imagine his giant cock in *there*. "I'm not ready for that," I complained, turning to face him. He held up his hands, yelling, "Don't point a loaded gun at me! Keep it on the target, for fuck's sake!"

"Oh, sorry," I pivoted to face forward again and aimed the pistol at the target.

"You want to keep your eyes open, put that white dot on the front sight right between the two white dots of the rear sight. Focus your eyes on the front sight, and not on the target."

"What? I can't see the target if…"

"Yes you can. Do it, aim it down at the target, and focus your eyes on the front sight."

I held the rough plastic of the pistol out in front of me, my eyes focusing on the white dot of paint on the little black square of the front sight.

"See? Look at the sight and you can still see the black shape of the target just fine, even though it's a little out of focus."

He was right, I could still see the target behind it, but it felt really unnatural.

"Okay, the last thing is pulling the trigger. Don't jerk the trigger back, pull it smoothly all the way back until it stops. Don't anticipate the kick-back of the gun, just hold it steady and smoothly pull the trigger." Rex demonstrated with his handgun, holding it in one hand out toward the target while looking at me.

BANG! I flinched at the surprise of the sound of his pistol going off. He was smiling, eyes twinkling from behind his tinted shooting glasses.

"Just like that, Penny. You want to be surprised when it goes bang. If you try to anticipate, you'll end up missing the target."

"Good, now with the safety off, point at that target down there of the body and aim for the center of his chest."

"Oh, I couldn't shoot at a person…"

"Penny, for fuck's sake, it's a piece of paper."

"I know, but…it feels creepy." I lowered the ready-to-fire gun down to point at the dirt.

"Would it feel creepy to shoot the mother fucker if he was about to rape you? Kill you? Make you wish he'd killed you?"

"No, I…You're so negative."

He shook his head. "Penny, you have no idea how dark this world can be. Shoot that goddamn target."

"Shouldn't I aim for a limb to immobilize him first?"

"Tell you what, Princess—if you can do that, go right ahead. I've been shooting for over twenty years, and I *still* don't have the skill to aim so well under stress that I can shoot a moving guy in the arm. So, no—if you try that, you're probably going to miss. If you're willing to aim a gun at someone and pull the trigger, you've already decided they have to die in order for you to live. Shoot to kill, not to injure."

"Okay, okay—but why then not aim for the heart?" Rex intimidated me, but I wanted to understand.

"The biggest area to aim for that will do the most damage is the center of the torso," he thumped the center of his muscular chest with his fist. "Aim here, the center of mass of the body. This is your first time, baby, you'll be lucky to hit anywhere near that damn target. Shit, you'll be lucky to keep the fucking bullet in South America."

"Fine," I snapped, pointing the firearm at the paper target.

"Now or never..." I took a deep breath and pulled the trigger smoothly. Before I knew it, with a crack the gun went off, the sharp jolt as it fired pushing me back before I regained my grip. "Did I hit it?"

"No, Penny. You closed your eyes when you pulled the trigger."

"I did?"

"It's a subconscious thing, like a flinch. All new shooters do it. Concentrate on keeping your eyes open and looking at the target even after the shot goes off. Now, shoot again."

I aimed again, holding the dot of the front sight on the black silhouette of a man and slowly squeezing the trigger. *Keep your eyes open...*

BANG! The shot again took me by surprise, but this time I was looking at the target and I saw it gently sway back and forth. "I hit it!"

"We're not done yet. Again!" Rex snapped. I aimed and took a breath, held the front sight on the target, gently squeezed the trigger, kept my eyes open, and was surprised at the bang. I saw the target paper jolt again. This time I wasn't startled, in fact, it was starting to be fun now that I knew what to do and what was going to happen. I continued to shoot until the weapon was empty, Rex holding up his hand in a stop gesture. "That was fun!" I couldn't help but be surprised at how good it felt to shoot.

He smiled. "See? Let's see how you did. Look and make sure the chamber is empty, then set the weapon down on the bench over there."

I did as I was told, and waited as he retrieved the target. "Do you need your glasses? Should I bring my younger eyes to look?" I teased as he shot back his middle finger to me.

He stared at the paper for a minute before turning to bring it back for me to see.

"Holy shit, Princess can shoot! Mother fuck— that's amazing."

He held up the target, riddled with bullet holes, most in the center in a cluster the size of my hand. He counted the holes. "All but two hit the target. I think he's dead. That's wicked good for a beginner, baby girl. Let me unload this round in mine, and we'll go back and play the way *you* wanted to."

"Can't we shoot all the bullets that you brought? What's that big rifle over there? Can I shoot that?"

He chuckled, shaking his head incredulously at me. "You surprise me every damn day," he said with a grin.

When we returned to the house, laughing and talking guns, Nate was standing at the door, arms folded, his lips pursed in his pissed-off Nate look. "I'm glad you two are having fun," he snipped.

"We were just...Rex taught me how to shoot, that's all."

"Thanks for asking me along." He tapped his foot.

"Quit acting like a jealous little bitch, Nathaniel." Rex's voice was firm, dismissive. "Come on, Penny, we have guns to clean."

"I, uh, I'll hang out with Nate," I said, looking to Nate, who would not make eye contact with me.

"You will fucking come clean your goddamn gun, and you'll do it now," Rex's voice boomed. He turned to walk toward a side room, guns in tow. I looked to Nate, confused, fighting tears. Being torn between them was more than I could bear. "Go, Penny," Nate finally said, turning to walk toward his room.

Nate's door slammed, and I scurried to the door where Rex was. Inside, the large room was set up to clean guns, and there was even a place to make, or maybe refill, spent bullets in the corner. "Here, I'll show you how to clean yours," Rex said as if nothing had happened. "You need to talk to him, to tell him... He's upset." He continued to clean his gun. "I'm not much for coddling people, sweetheart. We'll catch up with him later."

"Rex, I think..." He turned to face me, his massive frame hulking over me.

"You think what?" His tone was challenging.

"I think the three of us have a... We have a relationship, a beautiful one, and those take care and feeding." He took a deep breath. "Okay, go talk to him, I'll teach you this shit later."

"I-I think," he stared into me as I spoke. He was trying to intimidate me. "I think you should go talk to him, make an effort to… Just make some sort of effort… *Please*?"

"Mother fucker!" he shouted, "Stay here, don't touch *anything*."

I waited for what seemed like forever for Rex to return. I was terrified that today's spat, that today's episodes of jealousy, would tear us apart just as we were beginning. I needed *both* of these men—they were two halves making a whole for me.

Rex returned, without saying anything about Nate, and began his lesson on cleaning guns and preparing them for storage. I fought the urge to ask questions, instead completing my lesson to his satisfaction.

Hours later, Nate emerged from his room and sat across from me in the living room. "I'm sorry, I didn't mean to…I asked him if you'd want to…" He held a hand up to stop me. "No, I was being stupid. I *hate* target shooting. I felt jealous at you two being together doing something he loves and I don't. I was jealous…of *both* of you, really."

I placed my hand on his knee as he leaned in closer. "This isn't exactly the way things normally go when falling in love, is it?"

"Are you in love with me, Penny?" His steel blue eyes stared into mine, waiting.

"Yes."

"And him too?"

"Yes," I answered without hesitation.

"I'm in love with you both," he said, his hands raking through his hair. "Uncharted territory in so many ways, I guess some growing pains are to be expected?"

"He spoke to you?" I was desperate to know what happened between the two men.

"Uh huh," he nodded, a secretive smile crossing his lips.

"And?" I asked, yearning for more.

"And, we're all good. Plus, he reminded me that I have things to teach you, too. Things that I'm better at, like hand to hand combat."

"What?" I nearly fell off the couch.

"We both agree that to keep you safe, we have to teach you the skills to take care of yourself. It's tough out there, babe—we want to know that we've given you everything we have to give. It's important, Penny."

His words still rang in my ears... *Hand to hand combat—so much for my manicure!*

Chapter Six

That afternoon, after the guns were cleaned and Maria served lunch, I sat on the edge of Nate's bed as the two men stood in front of me. I was nervous—the primal look in Rex's eyes, the lustful need in Nate's, told me they wanted me. "Undress, Penny," Rex said with a snap of his finger. I stood, taking my new clothes off slowly and carefully laying them on the side of the bed. Rex loved the slow undress, and judging by the bulge forming in Nate's jeans, he did too.

"I have a challenge for you, Princess," Rex said. "Kneel in front of us." I did as he asked. "If you can make us both come at the same time, using your hands and mouth only, then we'll reward you with both of our tongues, at the same time, making you come." Nate licked his lips and glanced over to Rex—he craved us both. "But," Rex continued, "if we don't come together, then you won't be touched. Not by us, not by yourself. Do you understand?"

"Yes," I gulped.

My hands shook as I reached up to open the button-fly of Rex's soft jeans. Nate looked on lustily as I slowly pulled out Rex's thick cock, hardening as I stroked it. Experience with these men had taught me that Rex was a slow burner, his passion building in intensity with time, whereas Nate was more of a firecracker—bursting into multiple explosions without tiring. Since the challenge was to make them come *at the same time*, I decided to pleasure Rex until Nate couldn't take it much longer. The tip of my hungry tongue toyed with Rex's shaft, running along the piercings that ran across it, as he lengthened.

Nate groaned, his fingers brushing across his hard cock, uncomfortably contained in his snug jeans. "It has to be all her, bro," Rex said, nodding to Nate's fingers. Nate bit his lip, his face lifting toward the ceiling in an attempt to not watch the erotic display of me licking Rex's enormous cock. "Well played, Pen," Nate grunted as he gave up on the idea of not watching—the pull was too strong. His lusty eyes fed on Rex's cock being pleasured, my fingers stroking the swollen ridge emerging from the underside of his scrotum. Rex's muscled legs braced in a V, he was getting close to release. I reached for Nate's fly, unzipping his jeans and reaching into the soft cotton of his underwear to free his desperate cock. *"So ready,"* I mumbled. I wasn't sure if I was allowed to speak, but technically Rex said using my hands and my mouth—he didn't say in what capacity. I loved the physical differences between my two men—Rex was raw, natural, rough, whereas Nate was refined, smooth, groomed.

100

I kept my left hand grasped tightly to Rex's throbbing cock as I turned my oral attention to Nate's long, smooth cock—after a quick lick to his impeccably groomed balls. Nate was leaking salty fluid from his tip—it wouldn't take much to send him over the edge. I sucked him in rhythm until he was on the brink before moving my yearning tongue back to Rex, sucking him quickly down my throat the way he liked. I felt Nate twitch in my hands, and I knew it was time. I pulled Rex's cock, now hard as an iron bar, from my throat and let it rest just beyond my outstretched tongue. With both hands firmly stroking my two beautiful cocks, I let them both come all over my tongue—their orgasms so close they nearly rubbed the heads of their spewing cocks against each other.

I licked my lips before licking each man's spent fluid from their tips, craving more of them, but desperate to be allowed to come. "Well done, Princess," Rex's deep voice said washing over me. "On the bed, legs open, up against the pillows. I want you to be able to watch." I scurried to rest against the headboard, my neglected pussy dripping wet. Rex nodded to Nate, who crawled up to rest his head on my right thigh, his delicate nose sniffing at the scent of my arousal. "Go ahead," Rex growled as he positioned himself on the bed, against my left leg. "She's so fucking sweet," Nate said after the first swipe of his warm tongue along the delicate flesh of my pussy, his words vibrating against my engorged clit. The two men were side by side, I struggled to open wide enough for two faces until they decided to toss my legs over their shoulders, mercilessly opening me to their assault.

The two teased me, licking, flicking, penetrating, and sucking while I watched, being reminded more than once to open my eyes and enjoy the show. Rex's undiscriminating tongue licked me from my top to my virgin bottom, toying with me before moving back up to brush past Nate's tongue on my clit. Tongues together, as one, they licked at each side of my hard, swollen clit until I shook with pleasure. Still clenching, I begged them to fuck me—I needed to be filled. Nate's always-ready cock slammed into me, driving me to endless pleasure as Rex's tongue continued to mercilessly toy with my sensitive clit. When Nate was finished, Rex took over, fighting exhaustion to have me one more time.

We spent the week together, each night ending in three tangled, satisfied bodies sharing Nate's bed. I was sad the following week as Rex got ready to go back into the jungle. "I'm gonna miss you," I pouted as Rex gathered the last of his gear. He set down his heavy backpack, and turned to me. "I'll miss you like crazy, sweet Princess," he kissed me. "But I've got to work. Thanks to you, this group arrived flawlessly and happy—happy until I tear them down," he winked. "Keep running the office for me, and I'll keep in touch the best I can." I nodded, "I have some ideas for the next group's arrivals—I was thinking we could bring them to Medellin instead of Bogotá, save ground transport time and money." He smiled wide—that was the sort of detail work he hated. "I thought of that a while back, but the arrival lounge at Medellin is a bit ghetto." I grinned—I loved working with Rex. It kept my boredom at bay, and I felt useful, needed for the first time. And, I was actually good at it. "Yes, but you are going to rent your own arrival lounge—a plush one that I'll help you put together affordably. It's still far cheaper than bringing them into Bogotá." He reached for my chin, lowering his face to mine. "You're smart, Penny. How did I live without you?" We kissed goodbye as Nate walked in.

"Okay, Rex, Rodrigo has the van loaded with the gear, and the new recruits are headed to base camp. Kick ass and take names, man." Rex pulled on his heavy backpack and walked toward the door as we followed. "Have fun, my babies, but her virgin ass remains untouched, promise?" Nate nodded with a smirk. Rex's wide palm cupped the side of my face as he leaned in for one last kiss on my forehead. I expected him to give Nate his standard rustling of the hair and pat on the back, but instead he repeated the exact same gesture with Nate—palm of his hand to the side of Nate's angelic face, a quick peck of a kiss on his flawless forehead. Before we could process what just happened, he was gone.

We stared at the closed door for several long minutes. Nate eventually spoke, his fingers still on his forehead in the place Rex's lips had been. "Holy shit, did that just happen?" he asked incredulously. I nodded, unable to speak. "I'm never washing my forehead again," he joked.

Nate and I spent the week having sex, playing Xbox, having more sex, and training for the new badass-Penelope that the men wanted me to be. I was bruised from Nate trying to teach me how to escape from restraints. Unlike the shooting, I wasn't a natural at it in any way. Rex called twice, and it sounded like his week was going smoothly, without the complications I caused during his last survival course.

But, by the sixth day, I was bored. I decided to spend some energy preparing for Rex's return—I talked Maria into making his favorite foods, and I wanted to show off what I'd learned in his absence. As I looked through my outfits, I found the perfect dress to wear for him. Rex loved my curves to be wrapped in soft, billowy fabrics, so a gorgeous emerald green silk gown would be perfect. Except...it washed out my pale skin. With an idea in my impulsive head, I searched the expansive house until I found Nate.

"I need you to take me into town—I want to buy some makeup for Rex's welcome home."

He stared at me—my attempt at sounding casual didn't work.

He shook his head slowly from side to side. "No way—you can't leave the compound."

"Ugh!" I stomped my foot like a toddler. "Why?" I whined.

"You can't be recognized."

"Coolio—we'll disguise me. C'mon, *please*?" I tried to work the pouty lips on him.

"Penny," he sighed, "Rex will kill me."

"He won't know. I'm going crazy in the house! You both said I'm not a prisoner—I live here. I can leave here as I please, Rex said so himself."

"I'll go get you makeup, babe. The village isn't very big, there aren't many choices anyway."

"No, I want to pick it out. If you won't take me, I'll go alone." I crossed my arms. I meant it—I was getting out of the house for a few hours, no matter what.

"Penny, you're determined to get me into a lot of trouble. Come on, let's find a hat. I think the gardener is small; his clothes might fit you. Keep that blonde mane of hair under the hat, and don't take off the sunglasses."

Half an hour later, with my disguise in place, Nate drove us to town in a pickup truck used by the landscapers. The village was small—I'd never seen anything like it. There were fruit stalls, vegetable vendors, a man selling live chickens, and a few small mom and pop type shops littering a dusty main road. "This is it?" I asked incredulously. "Yeah, we live out pretty remote, but it's not that far to Medellin. That's where the plane is, and if we need more supplies than the town can provide, that's where we head. We also order stuff—delivery is pretty good. Your clothes came from Bogotá pretty quickly."

We parked the truck along the side of the road and walked along a dirt path toward a small drugstore. "This is it, babe—all the makeup in the village." We wandered the dusty store, the young woman behind the counter addressing Nate by name in English. "Juana, this is my cousin, James. Oh yeah, he's here to go to Rex's survival trek. Listen, we want to buy some cosmetics for a costume thing we're having." She smiled wide at Nate and scurried over, excited to have his attention and completely ignoring me. I pointed to a few things, and within fifteen minutes we were leaving the small shop with a paper sack full of drugstore makeup. I'd never been so excited about getting a ten dollar eyeliner in my life. In fact, I'd never actually worn a ten-dollar eyeliner.

"Happy now?" He slipped the paper sack into his rucksack. "Yes," I nodded, leaning up to kiss him before he held his hand up to stop me. "Whoa, cousin James," he reminded me. "Oops," I giggled. "Let's get some fruit salad," he said, guiding me across the street to a fruit stand. "That sounds too healthy," I moaned—I liked junk food. "Not this, you'll see."

"Do you speak much Spanish?"

"No, a few words here and there I've picked up. Rex is fluent, though."

We walked up to the rickety wooden fruit stall. I wasn't so sure I wanted to eat the food there. "Dos ensaladas de frutes, por favor," he said to the vendor. The man put two large scoops of ice cream in two Styrofoam bowls, covered them in cream, added chopped fruit, and finished the concoction with some sort of creamy cheese. He put a plastic spoon in each and, after Nate paid for them, handed them to us. I was skeptical, but the treat was delicious. "I'd eat this every day," I raved. "See? I'll confess I'm not a huge fan of Colombian food, but there are some gems." I took a big bite, and confessed, "I guess I expected tacos, margaritas, tortillas, and—"

"Penny, you do realize that Colombia is not in Mexico, right?"

"Yes, it's just—I guess I'm not very well traveled when it comes to Central or South America. I've been to Europe, but my parents usually left me with nannies when they traveled."

"I remember your mom," Nate said, "she seemed like a decent lady. I'm sorry you lost her so young."

"Me too," I said with sadness. "Mom was amazing, but my father never really seemed to have much use for me, and as she got weaker with illness, he had less and less use for her, too."

"That's horrible. Listen, Penny, I don't want to go into it here, but there's stuff about your father that you'll find out that will shock you. His business…Well, I'll just say he's involved in some pretty shady stuff."

"Is that why someone wanted me kidnapped and killed?" I asked him pointedly.

"Yes. I don't know the details, but I'm sure it's tied into your father."

We walked along the dusty road, eating our fruit salads and watching the kids play in the street. "What else is there to do here in the village," I asked, kicking a rock out of my path. "Well, there's a fight club up the hill."

"A what? Like in the movie?" I was shocked.

"No, it's more like a boxing gym, but they have a ring where guys will sometimes fight. The locals place bets, it's great practice—and you'll need practice soon."

"I'm *not* fighting anyone, Nathaniel, no fucking way."

He laughed and patted me on the shoulder. "No, cousin, of course not yet. I was teasing. Not as a boy, anyway. I wouldn't mind getting a round or two in before we go back, though."

I shook my head. "No, that's a really bad idea. Let's go on back…"

He grabbed my arm and tugged me to the end of the street, through a run-down fence, and down a long path strewn with garbage. At the end, a large metal building sat. It looked more like a massive industrial storage facility than a gym to me. "So you train here?" I asked nervously. "I've done some training with these guys, but I mostly come here to practice. A few quick rounds of bareknuckle, and back we go."

He knocked on the heavy metal door, and when a large man answered, he gave a password and we were allowed in. The place was hot—hot, wet, and reeked of sweat. I had to cover my nose to avoid vomiting. Nate pointed to a folding metal chair at the side of an elevated boxing ring surrounded by a metal wire fence. "Wait there," he instructed.

Nate walked over and talked to a skinny man who seemed to be in charge, who pointed to another man about Nate's size who was working out on a shredded punching bag hung from the ceiling with a chain. Nate nodded, and began to undress. My hand was still over my nose—the stench of the place causing the cream from the fruit salad in my stomach to churn.

A group of men, most dressed like cowboys and smoking cigarettes, gathered around the ring where Nate, stripped down to a pair of white boxer-briefs, and the other man, in a dingy pair of briefs that appeared to not have been washed in decades, prepared for their fight.

Taken by Two

The men placed their bets with a smoking man at a cash window, and stood around the ring. Nate and the man began to box, bare fisted, which quickly turned to kicking as well in some sort of mixed martial arts type sport. The man, who the spectators called Tito, got a good kick into Nate's face, and his nose bled as they continued to fight. The sight of bright red blood flowing down Nate's perfectly chiseled face upset me, and I worried about our safety as the men became louder and more aggressive.

The fight seemed to me to go on forever, with Nate emerging as the superior fighter. Tito flailed, and threw constant kicks and punches, but Nate was more of a tactician and waited to get the most impact from his efforts. As the fight drug on, Tito was visibly tiring. The throng of men howled and jeered, shouting at Tito—they'd bet on him and weren't happy about losing. I stood up from the metal chair as the men got more animated and angrier. I crept to the door and stood facing the ring. I felt the hair on the back of my neck stand up even though it was steamily hot in the gym. We were in danger, and I was ready to run. If I had a cell phone, I'd have called Rex for help.

Nate's designer underwear was coated with blood, but it was Tito's blood. With a solid hit to his nose, the man fell and didn't get up. I was relieved; it was nearly over. Until—another man walked into the ring. Fully clothed, wearing heavy cowboy boots, he swung at Nate, hitting him hard across the cheek, blood spurting from the cut. The gang of men didn't care about the rules—they were going to beat the shit out of the rich white American. I screamed for Nate, begged them to stop, but the fight continued. Nate was holding his own, but I was horrified of what would happen if Tito stood up.

Someone suddenly grabbed my behind roughly, and I turned around and swung, my fist landing in what felt like iron. "I'd know that bodacious ass anywhere, Princess," the low baritone of Rex purred in my ear. "Oh my God, Rex, I'm so glad you're here!" I'd never been so relieved in my life. "Uh huh, you won't be glad when I spank your ass red-raw later. What the fuck were you thinking!" His eyes were dark, ominous—his jaw set in a hard line—he was pissed. "Be angry, do whatever, but please save Nate. They are cheating! They added a second fighter—look, the new guy is wearing shoes!"

Rex looked around me toward the ring, his face showing no emotion. Nate looked over and saw him, nodded to Rex as the blood from his cheek flowed. Rex nodded back and walked over to the cashier's window. "What are you doing? Will that guy stop the fight?" I chased after him. "I'm going to place a bet, make a few *pesos*, baby." Tears flowed down my cheeks. "You'd bet against Nate?" I couldn't believe this was the man I thought I loved, betraying the other man I loved.

Rex placed his bet in Spanish and stood by my side, his arm forced around my waist despite my resistance. "I told you, Princess, I don't *rescue* people. This isn't my fault—you two did this. Doesn't have a fucking thing to do with me."

He stood there stoically, holding me as I struggled to squirm out of his arms. He repulsed me at the moment—I didn't know who he was. He ignored me and watched the fight. As I'd feared, Tito stood up.

Nate fought both men, but the tide had changed. He was on fire, unstoppable. "Oh my God! He's so good!" Rex let a tiny grin creep to the side of his mouth before giving me a quick squeeze. "Like Mark Twain said, 'It's not the size of the dog in the fight, it's the size of the fight in the dog.' Nathaniel Slater is fucking full of fight, sweetheart. So are you, so am I. Those two other guys? They're tired, weak."

The crowd jeered and eventually sat down in disgust as both of their men were knocked out by Nate. The manager of the gym walked into the ring, lifting Nate's hand to pronounce him the winner, and handing him a towel to wipe the blood. Nate dressed and walked toward us, his eyes anxiously on Rex. "Man, I–I fucked up," he said, waving his arms before raking his hands through his hair. "You fucked up *big time*. Let me collect our winnings, and we'll go."

After Rex left the window, shoving a wad of bills in his pocket, the throng of men crept over, angry and ready to start trouble, until Rex held up a gun and spoke to them in Spanish, pointing toward the door. They didn't move as we left the gym. The minute the door closed, Rex and Nate broke into a run, Rex picking me up when I couldn't keep up.

We made it to the truck. Rex's dark van, the one I'd been taken from the airport to the compound in, was parked behind it with Rex's driver idling the engine. "Get in," he screamed as the sliding door slid open. Nate and I jumped in, with Rex behind us slamming the door closed. He tapped the glass to tell the driver to go.

"I can't deal with you two right now—if I do, I'll fucking strangle you both. I have to get back to the jungle," he said through gritted teeth, not making eye contact with either of us. I held a towel to Nate's bleeding face, trying to calm myself down. I knew this was my fault—*me and my damn makeup*.

"How'd you know?" Nate asked, less afraid of Rex than I was.

Rex didn't look at him, but eventually answered, "DEA buddy of mine saw you two in town and called me. You're fucking lucky I had a signal."

"I could have handled Tito *and* Deke," Nate said defiantly.

The van was silent until we pulled into the tall walls of the compound, the security staff at the gate waving us in. Rex knocked on the glass, and the driver lowered it. "Tell them we need a couple of guys to go get the gardener's truck from town."

We left the van, Rex telling his driver he needed to leave for the jungle again as soon as he stitched Nate up.

"Wait, stitches?" I shouted to Rex's back as I followed him inside. "Shouldn't we go to a hospital, an ER, for that?"

Both men ignored me as we followed Rex through the house. At a far wing, he stopped at a heavy metal door, armed with a keypad and a small screen. He held his hand up to the screen, and when it beeped, he entered a code—his keystrokes shielded by his other hand. The heavy door slid open.

Inside, there was a brightly lit, windowless medical room. There were two gurneys, and the walls were lined with locked cabinets and medical equipment. "Welcome to the emergency room on King Rex Island," he said sarcastically. Nate hopped up onto one of the tables as if he'd been in this room many times before. Rex ignored me, walking over to a sink to scrub his hands. "It's on his face—should we get a plastic surgeon?" I once had a similar cut from a gymnastics fall and my parents went berserk about scarring. "What the fuck planet do you live on, Penelope? Go play with your makeup while the men get shit done," Rex said as he pulled on latex gloves. His words stung—I understood his anger at me, but I didn't know how to make it better. I slumped into a chair in the corner. Nate looked over at me and mouthed the words, "It's okay." I suspected he'd dealt with a much-angrier Rex before.

"Okay, dude, this isn't going to feel great, but once it's numb, I'll sew you up. I'm going to give Penny only enough codeine to get you through until I get back."

"No meds, no numbing."

"Nate, I appreciate that, I do." Rex's voice was soft, loving again. "The shot is just some lidocaine, it's not addictive. You can do over the counter Motrin after if you'd rather not risk opiates."

"Just the numbing shot, then, if you think it's okay—if not, I'll take the pain. But nothing after, no pills."

Rex nodded as he swabbed Nate's cheek with an alcohol swab, Nate grimacing from the sting. "I'd rather have you still when I sew—I'd hate to mar that pretty-boy skin," Rex said as he raised the needle. Nate showed no sign of pain as Rex gave the injection.

After Nate was numb, it took only minutes for Rex to have him sewed up. "Keep it clean and dry, and use this ointment. Your face will be fine—the rest of you maybe not so much when I get back from the jungle." He pulled off the gloves, tossed them in a stainless steel garbage bin, and gestured for us to leave.

We stood in the main living room waiting for Rex. He eventually emerged from the medical room and walked past us without a word. With a slam of the front door, he was gone. I looked to Nate, battered, bruised, and stitched. "He's so mad—he's never going to forgive me," I cried to Nate, who held me as we walked back to his bedroom. "He gets that way—believe me, Pen, I've done *far* worse things to make him *much* madder than this. It'll pass, just weather the storm."

Later that evening, with no word from Rex, I sat out by the pool having dinner with Nate. "How's the face?" I asked, sipping a glass of chilled white wine as Maria cleared the dishes. "Hurts, but my whole body aches. The sign of a great fight."

I shook my head at him. "I don't get it—that didn't seem like sport to me. When they added that second guy to the ring…"

"Oh, that group always fights dirty. That's their thing—I knew it was coming. I wanted to play them. The gym manager, Chewy, would have stopped it otherwise. I placed a bet on myself with him before the fight."

"Going there was careless, I have to side with Rex on this one. I was an idiot for not listening to you when you said no to going to town, and you were an idiot for taking me," I admitted.

He took a small sip of his glass of wine. Despite battles with drug addiction, Nate wasn't much of a drinker. "Well, Penny, I don't have the best judgment. I'm rash, impulsive. Rex is good for me in that regard. He's taught me to slow down, strategize, *think*. And most importantly, when you fuck up, you pull *yourself* back together and start again. *Never* stop fighting. Today was a set-back, nothing more." I leaned back into my chair, the stars dancing overhead as the warm, wet air wrapped around me like a hug.

"You met Rex when you took his course?" He nodded. "My dad talked to me into it—but he's a whole other story. I'd just come out of yet another ninety-day rehab and was looking for something different. I showed up, pampered and arrogant, and ended up leaving Rex's 'let's eat wild animals' shit after the first day. I managed to hitch my way to Medellin, where it was easy to score plenty of cocaine by just signing my name. Well, it was for a day or so. When I couldn't pay—all of my stuff was back in Rex's airport storage—the dealers got pissed. In the back of a dank warehouse, I was given two options: pay my hefty drug bill, or they'd slowly cut me into pieces. Starting there," he pointed grimly to his groin.

"Oh my God," I gasped. "What did you do?"

"They let me make a phone call—no way in hell I was calling dear ol' dad, so I dialed Rex's Blackberry." He smiled and shook his head. "Looking back now, I was lucky as fuck that it connected! The signal out there is beyond sketchy."

"So you called Rex and he came and rescued you?"

"No, he hung up on me. Told me in order to survive, I needed to learn to unfuck things for myself."

"That's harsh."

"You know by now King Rex can be harsh. Harsh *and* cold. But, he did send one of his buddies, one of the spook-type agents he used to work with, over with my belongings, including my wallet. The guy helped me pay off the dealers and, clueless as to what to do with me, dropped me back with Rex. By the time I got to the compound, I was already crashing from the binge. Rex locked me in the safe room—where you stayed at first—as I suffered through the pain. At some point, in the throes of delirium and hallucinations, I started screaming for 'daddy'—I have no idea where *that* came from. But, for some reason, it made an impact on him. He came in and held me all night long—physically held me in a bear hug for hours because it was the only thing that would calm me down."

"I know why that made an impact—he told me about his father."

Nate gulped and nodded. "Yeah, that's rough stuff. My own dad—I mean, he *thought* he was doing the right thing, but I just can't forgive him. Rex thinks I should, but Penny—he called the cops on me! He turned me in—more than once."

"Tough love?"

Nate refused to answer, and we sat there in silence as the jungle howled around us outside the secured walls. It did feel like an island here, the compound. I could see why Rex jokingly called it King Rex Island.

"I think that's where my physical attraction to him began—it sprang from that night, being calmed and soothed by his touch." Nate's voice was soft, his face shrouded in the darkness of the night. "The next day, he told me about his own father, and then said he'd never shared that with anyone before, not even his wife. We were both shocked at the connection we had, but, for some reason, the universe brought us together and we just bonded. Bonded *hard*."

"So you stayed?"

"Sort of. I went home, did another ninety-day program. My dad tried to sue to have me deemed incompetent so he could run my business for me. That's the last time I spoke to him. Rex is convinced he was just trying to gain control of my money so I couldn't use, but I don't know. I just can't get over it. I mean, Rex runs my money for the same reason."

"But you made that decision, right? *You* asked Rex to do that?"

"Yes—that's the difference. Rex doesn't make decisions for me—like he says, he doesn't *save* people. He gave me the tools to save myself—or at least try to. I'm still working on it, but I'll get there."

"So your dad talked you into coming back to Colombia?"

"No! He actually bitched and moaned about Rex running a course for addicts in a place where drugs are rampant. He wanted to sue Rex for my binge." He shook his head and sighed, "Penny, drugs are rampant everywhere. There's no place in the world I can't score cocaine—I've even done it *in*

117

rehab. I came back on my own, and did my week in the jungle—and discovered for the first time that I *am* strong. I *can* conquer my demons. I don't need anyone to rescue me, and not even addiction can hold me down."

I smiled. That was exactly the life-changing experience I had during my brief stay with Rex in the jungle.

"I did the course, and rocked it. I even went back for a few of his advanced ones. I didn't want to go back to an office in Silicon Valley after fighting for my survival in the Amazon—I set it up so I could stay here, with Rex, and disappear from public life. All the parties, women, events—it all just seemed so shallow and pointless after being here."

I understood exactly what he meant. "Your father knows you're here?"

He nodded. "Yeah—and he doesn't give me any grief since I've stayed clean. He conceded to Rex a few months ago that Colombia is best for me. I don't know—they talk or whatever, but I still won't."

"So you've been clean ever since the binge?"

He chuckled, running his long index finger along the rim of his glass. "I've had a few setbacks...but I'll make it."

"I've been happy here, but something was missing," he continued. "The whole platonic thing left me craving intimacy. After his wife left, Rex didn't want to be with anyone. I, however, wasn't going to be sexless for long. I tried hooking up a few times, but it felt empty to me. I really wanted to be with *him*, but he was never going to feel the same. He tried to give me affection as he could bring himself to, to make me happy, but until we found you, I was restless, lonely. I love him, and I love you, Penny. You complete the circle—loving you makes us complete."

"You never even asked me out before...I'm not sure we ever even spoke to each other?"

"No, but I always felt a chemistry with you— like you were a kindred spirit. Which, of course, I avoided. I suspect you did, too. But when I heard you were in danger, it clicked. I knew you had to be with us."

"Except, now Rex hates me." My heart hurt at the thought of him being disappointed in me.

"He doesn't," Nate said with finality.

The next day, I waited for Rex's return like an errant child waiting for dad to get home from work. Nate, however, was calm about it. "We'll take our lumps and move on," was his advice to me as we cuddled in his warm bed that morning. "What if he makes me go," I worried. His blue eyes softened as his fingertips ran across my chin. "That won't happen, babe. It'll work out."

Rex blew in like a hurricane at three that afternoon—an angry hurricane. He dropped his gear, leaving it for Maria and the driver to clean and put away. Ignoring me, chasing after him apologizing, and Nate, who quietly sat in a chair reading, he stormed into his office and slammed the door. "I guess he's still a tad bit peeved," Nate joked with a raised eyebrow.

I did the administrative work for Rex's business, and I had plenty of reasons to be in his office. "I have work to do in there," I said out loud to no one in particular. But, he'd locked the door, and didn't answer my incessant knocking. "Give him time, Pen," Nate said from the corner. "Let's go work on your fighting skills—but go easy on my stitched up face."

Rex never emerged from the cocoon of his office, and once again Nate and I had dinner together, without him. Maria took Rex's meal to him on a tray. Later that evening, I leaned against Nate's firm chest in his giant porcelain egg shaped tub, surrounded by luxurious bubbles. "Why don't you go to him, Pen? Put on that green gown—I always give him space, maybe your way is different."

I thought about what he said. "I'll try."

"But wash off the eyeliner first," Nate teased.

It was nearly eleven before I gathered the courage to make Rex acknowledge me. I rapped on his door, nothing. I tapped again, drumming my fingers on the wood in a lively tune until he roared, "Go away!"

"I'm not leaving. In fact, I'm about to start singing Taylor Swift songs, followed by your favorite, Justin—"

The door flung open, my fingers left waving in mid-air.

"Stop," he said. He stood in front of me, a billowy linen shirt over his tanned skin, unbuttoned so that the muscles of his torso and the dusting of golden hair along his ribs and down from his navel distracted me. His hair was messy, flopping over his forehead. He punched his hands into the pockets of his favorite worn, ripped jeans that ended above his bare feet. "I can't take it anymore," I begged, my voice barely above a whisper. "Sit," he said, pointing to the edge of his bed.

I walked past him and perched on the edge of his king-sized bed as he locked the door. Rex knelt in front of me, his eyes looking into mine. "Are you going to make me leave?" I asked when he said nothing.

"No."

"I'm so sorry—I made a mistake. It was *me*, though. I talked Nate into it. I will never disobey you again."

"Nate's easy to talk into mischief. He knew better than to take you out. I'm mad at him, *crazy* mad, but nobody is going anywhere." I took a deep breath in relief.

"But you, Penny, all I can think about is what if something happened to you. There are people who want you *dead*. You've become…I mean, to me you are…" He abandoned words and wrapped me in his strong embrace, holding me tight against his chest. I clung to him, never wanting him to let me go. "I'm sorry, Rex. I-I'll do better, I swear. I love you so much…"

He pulled back sharply and stared at me. "Penny, I'm not the kind of man you should love, I—"

"But I do. Nate does, and I do. I'm in love with both of you."

"Shit, Princess, you've captured me wholly. The two of you…I'm yours…"

The tough man inside fought the mist of tears that threatened to break his cold exterior. I pulled him closer to me, my arms clawing at him until he pulled us both into his bed. I couldn't get close enough to him. I looked around his room—I'd never been in there before, we all usually slept in Nate's room. The décor was almost identical to his office—deep brown leathers, dark mahogany woods, and survival equipment lining the walls. His bed was simple—comfortable linens in ivory and chocolate colors.

"The thought of losing you *wrecks* me, baby." His lips found mine, the kiss so soft, so loving, it barely seemed the Rex I'd come to know. Gentle touches pulled down the silk straps of the silky gown, his warm lips delicately toying with a breast before moving down. For the first time, he *made love* to me—his eyes on mine, his caresses gentle, and his thrusts slow and lingering. We were together like that for hours—the cervix-bruising man who left my lips swollen, my nipples throbbing, and my pussy aching was temporarily replaced by the Rex who wanted to show me how much he cared for me, despite not being able to say the words.

Still inside of me, his heavy body on top of mine as I dozed off to an exhausted sleep, he said the words I didn't expect to ever hear from him: *I love you.*

I woke up sometime later, his naked body lifting mine in his powerful arms. "What's wrong?" I yawned. "Nothing, Princess, everything is right." He carried me half-asleep across the house to Nate's room, pushing the door open with his foot. Nate was awake—sitting in a chair with his head in his hands. When he saw us, the veil of confusion clouded his sad expression. "Something was missing," Rex said to him, laying me down gently in the middle of Nate's sprawling bed. "*Someone* was missing, come to bed," Rex said, reaching a hand out to Nate.

The terror of what could have been faded that night as we embraced what was—the breathtaking splendor of three people finding each other in the blackness of the universe. I faded to sleep nestled between the two men who meant the world to me—the two men I loved more than anything.

The next morning, we were a tangle of limbs who'd spent the night fighting for Nate's covers. Rex and Nate were fast asleep, but I had to pee. Rex's heavy leg, one of the few places on his body that wasn't tattooed, rested across mine. The sleeping Nate's leg was across me from the other side, butted up against Rex's in peaceful cohabitation. If I had a camera, I would have taken a picture of the three of us intertwined physically and emotionally—it was a beautiful thing.

Chapter Seven

"Well, Princess, how do you feel about sucking chest wounds?" Rex asked over breakfast, his eyes never leaving his morning paper.

"Um, excuse me?" I blurted out, the mouthful of eggs I was chewing suddenly not so appealing.

"Oh," he glanced up, reaching for his mug of strong, black coffee. "I meant some medical training—simple stuff, first aid type of thing. Out here, you're often not close to a good doctor. It's part of teaching you to thrive here with us."

"Personally, I try to stay *very* close to a good doctor..." Nate piped in from his perch on the leather stool next to me, his lopsided grin fading as Rex glared at him.

"Good? I'm fucking *great*. But seriously, Penny, we need to give you the tools to really take care of yourself. No more floating through life on auto-pilot."

"Got it, but can we talk about sucking wounds after breakfast?"

Nate's grin returned, as he quipped, "I wouldn't mind some sucking after breakfast." Maria shot him a sharp glare and cleared her throat. "Sorry," Nate apologized. "You Catholics are so uptight…"

"I'm not Catholic," I answered.

"King Rex is."

I thought back to his tattoos—*the Virgin Mary, the cross at the very center of his chest, over his heart…* "Can we give this topic a rest?" Rex's deep voice scolded from behind his newspaper.

Before I'd even had time to digest my eggs, my diligent men had me outside the compound, near where we usually did target practice. "Why out here?" I whined, "It's so sticky and hot—I can learn first aid in the air conditioning!"

Rex sighed as Nate rolled his eyes at me. I was prone to complaining, but after I got a whine or two out of my system, I did usually focus on the lesson they were trying to teach me. "Outside is most likely where you'll find yourself, or someone else, injured with no access to medical care. Now, I don't have dummies or anything to practice on, so I brought out this dummy." Laughing at his own joke, he pointed to Nate. Rex rarely tried to be funny, but occasionally when he did he found himself far more humorous than anyone else.

"Okay," he continued, irritated that no one laughed at his dummy joke but him, "with a bullet wound, you want to do three things quickly—stop the bleeding, treat any symptoms of shock, and keep the patient breathing."

He pointed to the ground, indicating where he wanted Nate to pretend to be shot.

"Always, *always*, have your first aid kit with you. Never leave this compound without the backpack we put together the other day."

"Yes, sir," I agreed.

"So, the first order of business is stopping the bleeding as quickly as possible. Most gunshot victims die from bleeding out. The best way is with pressure and a clotting agent. In your bag, you have both Celox and a Quick Clot pack. For a big wound," he knelt down next to Nate, who was playing dead, and reached to unbutton his shirt. Nate, always a clown, emitted a long, erotic moan. Rex ignored him, and pulled open his shirt, marking a large circle on Nate's perfectly toned chest with a Sharpie. "What the fuck Chuck!" Nate sat up, looking down at his chest. "That's the bullet wound, unless you'd rather I give you a real one for her to learn on?"

"You couldn't use something washable? I work hard on these washboard abs!" Nate was rubbing at the impervious marker imprint.

"You could *use* some ink on that virgin, pasty chest. Washboard abs?" Rex lifted his black t-shirt and pointed at his own ripped torso. "*These* are fucking washboard abs and, at my age, I have to work twice as hard to get them!"

"Can we finish this please? I'm sweating." I'd had enough of the male pissing contests that always seemed to erupt.

Nate flopped back into the thick grass in a pout as Rex continued drawing the imaginary bullet wound on his skin.

"First thing, stuff that bleeding mother fucker with the clotting pad, then do antibiotic gel where you can, like this," he demonstrated on the imaginary wound, "followed by pressure. I mean *hard* pressure."

I knelt on the spongy grass next to Rex, making mental note of the order of steps.

"After the blood is stopped, you apply the pressure bandage. You don't want to just bandage up a gushing wound—the patient can bleed out and you won't notice because of the bandage. And don't go fishing around for the bullet like in the movies—stop the blood, get it sanitary, and wrap that sucker up."

I nodded. With Nate playing dead on the ground, the lesson seemed too real—my joking turned to serious attentiveness.

"Pressure bandage," he pulled one out of my backpack, "will aid in stopping the bleeding only if it's applied tight enough. It's key that the pressure be strong enough to fully stop the bleeding while the clot pack does its job. Make sense?"

I nodded, unwrapping the bandage.

"While getting the bandage on, you'll need to apply strong pressure with your hands and maybe tape if you have it. It's important, Penny—no time to be delicate, which is why we aren't going to practice the pressure on Nate—too easy to break a rib. But, when it's the real thing, give that fucking wound everything you've got. Apply as much pressure as it takes to stop the bleeding."

"There's tape in my emergency kit," I confirmed, riffling through it.

"Always, duct tape is useful *everywhere*. You also have Super Glue for smaller cuts."

"What if the wound is too big for the Quick Clot pad? Like in Tarantino movies where they get blown away with a shotgun and the wound is spewing?"

"Ah," Rex nodded, delighted that I'd been paying enough attention to ask a relevant question. "In that case, you'd try a tourniquet—we'll cover that tomorrow. I think that's enough for today. I need to hit the Crossfit hard this afternoon—got to work on *my* washboard abs." He reached down and pinched at Nate's tummy, causing Nate to writhe in ticklish laughter.

"I think the patient will live," he teased, continuing to tickle Nate.

After dinner that evening, we had drinks on the large balcony attached to my room. Nate and I shared a bottle of wine, while Rex sipped his standard tumbler of bourbon. "This room...it's the same as when..." I took another gulp of wine for courage. "It's the same as when she..."

"She left, Penny, you can say it. And, you can say her name. I'm good with it, honestly. The past is fading into the past. *That* Evelyn, the one I knew, is long since dead. Her grief and addiction has taken her over—she's someone else now."

"Addiction?"

"Yes," he took a deep breath. Rex wasn't one to share much, but he was little by little letting me, and Nate, in. "I brought her here to try to save her from her grief. Well, her grief drove her to drugs, which drove her to *him*."

"Him?" I asked.

"Pablo Lazar," Nate answered for him as Rex sipped his bourbon. "She left Rex for someone who could hook her up with drugs—they're married now. Last time I saw her, in Bogotá, it was like she was a ghost—vacant, dead stare..." Nate shook his head as if the memory was distasteful.

Rex took another gulp and reached over and grasped our free hands together. "I didn't mean to bring up pain, I was mostly wondering if I could change some things in this room? Make it more my taste?" I nodded my head toward the French doors leading into the room I occupied, even though I always slept with both men in Nate's bed.

"Oh, sure, yeah—but you're not leaving here to shop."

"I can pick out some things online—I'll pay. Or, I mean...I guess I don't exactly have access to my funds..."

Nate smiled. "I'm loaded, Pen, don't worry about it. And, King Rex is a lot wealthier than he projects in those same shredded jeans and tired black t-shirts every day."

Rex glared at him. "Sorry I'm not sporting designer hipster jeans in the jungle like the male model here."

"I like you both dressed exactly as you are," I put my drink on the table and slid a hand across Nate's knee, "and I don't want to leave here, ever. But, shouldn't I tell my dad I'm okay? They'll be wondering, right?"

The two men shared a guilty look before Nate began to speak, his hand on my arm, his voice soft, his words carefully chosen.

"Penny, your father is the reason someone tried to hire Rex to kill you." I sat still and absorbed the meaning of his words.

"Dad wants me dead?"

"No, but David Sedgewick is deeply involved with the cartels, with the drug trade. He launders cash through the casino, and they reward him for it."

I was stunned. I knew dear ol' dad wasn't father of the year—but involved with *drug cartels*?

"Are you sure?" I couldn't put any other words together. They sat silently, allowing me to absorb the news, before Rex continued.

"We're sure, Princess. He has been for years. A lot of my work…Well, I'm very familiar with the DEA, let's just say. His rival, Stewart Lynn, is the one who sent his henchman to hire me. The plan was to kidnap you, then make it look like you overdosed here in Colombia—blame the cartels and your father in a big public display."

"Yeah…" I was incredulous. "Lynn is a bitter rival and running for office soon." I was stunned.

"I'm sure someone else was hired when I refused. I don't know who took the job—until I do, and neutralize that, you need to stay hidden."

"Why would Lynn try to hire *you*?"

"He has contacts at the DEA, I'm guessing he figured that since I was out now, doing private business… That's really all I can say."

"Do you…do *that*?"

"No, baby, I don't." I was relieved to hear that, at the very least.

Chapter Eight

"Penny, come here." Rex's rich voice drew me to him, but I was stubborn. "No, just drink your drinks and smoke your smokes. I'll just hang over here with my friends—oh wait, I don't have any." Rex leaned into Nate, the orange glow from the end of the fat cigar in his left hand flaring as he brought it to his lips and puffed. They were close, their legs touching as they sat on the stone bench in Rex's garden at the side of the house. Nate leaned in even closer, his lips whispering something into Rex's ear, causing a raucous belly-laugh from Rex. *They are making fun of me.*

I'd been at the compound with the two men for the prior two weeks, and we'd grown closer. I felt like this was the home I'd always craved, but never knew existed. At times, however, I had growing pains from the sudden infusion of life with two men. In Vegas, partying and having random sex with lots of men was common, but I'd never lived with one. I was an only child, and my father was never around our day-to-day life. With Rex and Nate, however, I often felt like I'd been tossed into a frat house. I didn't always understand them, and sometimes felt left out. The tension was magnified by the fact that I was younger. Nate was in his late twenties and had been on his own running a business for years, and Rex was in his forties—stubborn and set in his ways. At twenty-four, I definitely had a lot of growing up to do.

Minutes prior to my storming off in a huff, Nate had told a joke. A joke I didn't understand. "Hey Pen, what's the square root of sixty-nine?" I, of course being decent at math and not getting that it was a joke, answered, "Uh, eight something, I'd need a calculator." The men burst into peals of ridiculous laughter, and I felt targeted—ridiculed. My entire life, despite being a good student, I'd been treated like a dumb blonde. That night, my insecurities crushed down on me, and I made a mountain out of a molehill. As the men laughed at what I later understood to be a joke from Nate, the punch line being, "Ate something," a sexual innuendo, I took it far too personally. I flew out of my chair, tossing my wineglass into the lush lawn, and raced toward the house.

"Fuck you both!" I howled at them as I made my hasty retreat. Rex's head snapped toward me as I yelled at them.

"Penelope, if you act like a child, I'm going to treat you like a child." His tone was stern, but Nate was laughing as he sipped his bourbon.

"You do anyway!" I turned to leave, but paused at the path to the house. I hoped one of them would chase me, preferably Nate.

"Oh do I?" I stood still, listening for footsteps behind me.

"Penny, come here," he commanded once again, his voice serious.

"No." I stood on the path facing the house.

"Okay, if that's what you want—I'll show you how a child is treated."

I heard the men rise, Nate's giggling now gone quiet. The curiosity was too much, and I turned to face them. Rex snuffed out his cigar in the heavy ashtray, and Nate followed suit.

Rex looked directly at me, the crystal tumbler of liquor in his right hand. "Come here or I'm going to spank that perfect ass."

"You wouldn't!" I squealed, my insides quivering in both fear and anticipation.

"Oh, Princess, I would!" He set the glass down and started toward me in long strides. I turned and ran toward the house, but Rex was too fast. In seconds he had me over his shoulder, like a sack of potatoes, and was carrying me into the house.

Nate chased after us, calling to Rex, "Hey, hey, let's slow down a minute…uh…"

"Slow down? I think your firm ass might be reddened to match hers."

"Oh," Nate answered, his words dripping with lusty need.

The anger dissipating, I smacked playfully at Rex's back as he hauled me through the house, my billowy mini-skirt floating up to reveal my bare butt cheeks, my lacy thong leaving plenty of skin exposed. By the time he deposited me on the center of the bed, I was in peals of laughter. Rex maintained his stone-cold demeanor as he sat on the edge of the bed. "Over my knee, Princess," he pointed to his lap.

I'd never been spanked—not as punishment, not erotically—never. But, I was no stranger to sexy BDSM books, and although I'm not into pain, the idea of Rex's giant hand across my bottom, with Nate watching, had me soaking my panties. "Hurry or I'll spank you harder," he barked. I crawled across the bed toward Rex. The room was lit only by the golden glow of the bedside lamp. Nate was crouched on the floor in front of us, his back against the wall. The glimmer of excitement was mixed with concern—I knew he wouldn't let anything happen to me that I didn't want. As Rex said, I didn't need one, but Nate would always be my knight in shining armor. As I positioned myself across Rex's powerful thighs, I winked at Nate and smiled. He nodded and licked his lips, leaning back against the wall, his legs parting into a wide V.

Rex lifted my skirt and pulled my tiny thong panties to the side. "*Fuck, Princess, you're dripping wet,*" he marveled, dipping a large finger inside me. He pulled it out, licked it, then slid it back in. I moaned a loud, wanton, "*Ah!*" as he pulled the finger out again. This time, he held it out to Nate. Without a word, Nate crawled over and sucked Rex's finger, covered in my slippery arousal. As Nate sucked, I could feel Rex harden beneath me, his cock pressing into my legs through his jeans. He made one last dip into my throbbing pussy, this time holding his withdrawn finger to my lips. "Suck," he commanded.

His large left palm spread across my ass, gently kneading, as I sucked my own fluid from his salty right index finger. "I'm going to pardon you, sweetheart," he said, pulling my skirt back down over my ass. "No," I blurted out, turning my face toward him. He smiled. "You're such a naughty girl, Penny—you *want* to be spanked?" I pushed my lower lip out, "Yes, please, I've been so very bad."

With a sigh, he said, "Okay," and raised my short skirt to my waist. "I do hope you remember your safeword, baby." *What safeword?* His large hand came down in a stinging swat. "Ow!" I wailed as he rubbed my reddening skin. "Enough?" I shook my head, "More." *Swat!* The second spank was harder, my other butt cheek radiating a stinging warmth as he caressed it. "Done?" I wriggled on his lap before muttering, "Nope." Four more fast spanks stung my ass in quick succession, then his comforting massaging fingers soothing the pain. Before I could think, he continued. A quick, sharp smack to my inner thigh, one to each burning butt cheek, one low across my emerging clit that caused me to moan and wiggle, and a fast slap across the very center of my ass before he grunted out, "Ready to say the safeword?" My hips gyrated as he spanked a few more times before I could form the words, "You never gave me a safeword!"

"Oh," he said with a chuckle. "That's because I'm not into that stuff, and I don't spank people. But, you sure as hell got turned on from a little slap-ass." Nate's eyes were wide from the floor, his hand rubbing his thick cock up and down through his jeans. "Who else here has been bad, Penny?" Rex tugged my skirt down over my red behind and pulled me up into his arms. "Nathaniel has been downright childish," I answered quickly. "What?" Nate looked confused, nervous…and turned on as hell. "Over my knee, bad boy—drop the pants and take it like a man."

Nate stood slowly. He looked to me, and as I nodded, he pulled his belt through the loops of his jeans. Tossing the thick leather belt to the floor, he yanked at the button on his jeans, unzipping them as we watched. In a single motion, Nate dropped his pants to his ankles, followed by the designer boxer-briefs. I took a deep breath in as I absorbed the beauty that was Nate naked. He slid his linen shirt off his shoulders, and placed it alongside his jeans before walking toward Rex.

"You don't want to fight for it?" Rex asked.

"No." Nate knelt on the floor next to Rex, his chest over Rex's knees. Nate's height didn't allow for the full straddle that I had done. "How childish has he been, Penny?"

Nate looked to me with a lascivious grin and winked, licking his lips. He was still rock-hard. "Five, I think," I answered, my eyes never leaving Nate's.

"Five it is." At the first swat from Rex's hand, Nate's eyes closed and he bit his lower lip. Not in pain, but in pleasure from the intimate position, from the sublime closeness of being hand spanked by Rex. "More?" Rex asked, ensuring the game hadn't gone too far. "Please," Nate husked. Four more luscious, loud spanks befell Nate's ass, his hips gyrating from the sting and the pleasure at the same time, his hard cock straining for contact with something to relieve it. "Well done," Rex barked as he rubbed the red marks he'd made on Nate's sculpted butt cheek.

"I think Penny is horny—she loved watching you. I don't think I'm done with her ass tonight, though." Rex motioned for Nate to lie back against the headboard before walking over to the nightstand drawer and pulling out a clear bottle of lube. "I told you I'd claim that ass, Princess. Now that it's warmed up is the perfect time. Face down on the bed, right there in front of Nate but don't touch him." Spanking excited me, despite my trepidation, and the thought of him entering my virgin asshole had the exact same effect. I'd grown comfortable with both men's fingers and tongues exploring me there, but I wasn't sure either man's thick cock would fit.

Rex dropped his pants, his huge erection breaking free. He quickly removed all of the metal from his cock except the barbell underneath. "I don't want anything to catch," he explained as I stared wide-eyed.

"I'm scared a little," I said meekly as Rex rubbed the warm, slippery lubricant all over my backside.

Rex's tone was softer as he said, "Don't be, you'll be in control, okay?"

"Uh huh," I muttered, unsure how I could have control flat on my stomach, with my ass in the air.

"Move up a little, on Nate's chest, yeah like that," Rex instructed. With my cheek on Nate's chest, his fingers caressing me, I instantly felt safer. Nate pulled me up to kiss him, and as our tongues intertwined, I felt the dull throb of being opened by Rex's thumb—I was used to that. He'd wait until I was comfortable and open before going any farther. Except, as the mild burn of being stretched faded, and I pressed for more, I realized with a loud, "*Ah!*" that it wasn't his thumb. "I'm stopping there, baby, that's enough for the first time," he soothed as his agile fingers reached around to stroke my clit. I pulled back from Nate's kiss, his fiery blue eyes searching my face. "No, I-I want more," I said in a near-moan.

"Push back when you're ready, you're driving, okay? I'm going to be still. But tell me when it's enough, don't just pull out fast."

"Uh huh," I whispered, pushing back for more. The feeling of being filled there was like nothing I'd ever felt before, and the combination of him stroking my clit at the same time was heavenly.

"Slide back down if you're ready—I think Nate's neglected cock could use some sucking."

The sensation of taking him like that, and being stroked and opened by his hand while I sucked on Nate was better than any sex I'd ever known. I climaxed over and over, clenching his swollen shaft as I shuddered—so far gone in my own ecstasy I wasn't conscious of them coming until Rex slowly pulled himself from me, Nate's salty come coating my tongue as my mouth struggled to hold on.

"Damn, girl, you're an ass-natural," Rex teased as I came down from the high of multiple orgasms. "I-I liked it, but it was only a little of…"

"Nope, Princess, you pretty much took that beast down to the balls slapping," he said, collapsing next to Nate as I crawled up to snuggle in between them. Rex pulled the fluffy comforter over us—we were too exhausted to move. Nate stroked my chin, his fingertips floating over my lips as we drifted off to sleep.

Chapter Nine

"*Crave Magma?*" I stood on the lush lawn across from an exasperated Nate.

"Krav Maga—it's sort of mixed martial arts, not what I do in the ring, but a great method for you to learn some basic self-defense type stuff that will work for you if threatened. It's not really the sport type of fighting I love." Nate was dressed simply—a gray t-shirt, workout shorts, with his feet bare. I was dressed nearly the same, despite my whining about wanting to wear sneakers—I'd just painted my toenails a bright red, and the idea of chipping them pissed me off.

"Can you teach me without hurting me?" I wasn't getting out of today's lesson no matter how hard I tried. Rex was in town restocking supplies, but made it clear before he left that he wanted to see progress when he returned that afternoon.

"I get learning self defense; I promise to concentrate. But, the attraction of sport fighting I don't get. You don't seem the type to get off on pain."

Nate shook his head. "I hate pain, Penny. I'm not like… Well, pain isn't my thing for sure. But, the fighting is a safe way for me to get the demons out. Before I started doing the mixed martial arts thing, for sport, cocaine fueled that rage. I've learned to fight it out when it builds up instead."

"You seem to have had a golden life, Nate—a great family, fairly normal middle-class upbringing, and a career that skyrocketed. I know about your mom's cancer, but other than that, why the rage?" Nate's mother battled cervical cancer, but she was in remission the last I heard from mutual friends.

He bit his lip and paled as he thought a moment before pointing toward a bench at the side of the lawn. "Let's sit," he said.

My leg rubbed against his on the stone bench as I waited for him to speak. I sensed I'd touched on something deep, and the knot in my gut told me I was about to finally understand what drove Nate to self-destruct. His palm rested on the top of my thigh as he began. "When I was nine, my teenage cousin moved in with us. His mother, my mom's sister Doreen, was going through an ugly divorce and couldn't handle things, apparently. Kyle moved into my room and…"

"Oh my God, did he…abuse you sexually? Is that why…"

"*What?*" Nate looked at me in horror. "Fuck no, that doesn't…" He took a deep breath as my eyes filled with tears. "I'm sorry, I'm just trying to understand," I whispered.

His hand caressed my leg. "It's okay, I didn't mean to snap. This isn't easy for me to talk about."

"I love you," I answered, squeezing his hand. "I'm here, you don't have to tell me more than you're comfortable with."

"It wasn't sexual," he clarified, his tone calmer this time. "My cousin Kyle was huge, and I wasn't. I've always been thin, but back then I was tiny—spindly, weak. He was a bully—he terrorized me for a year. It got so bad I started to…pee the bed, shake, I developed an eye twitch, that sort of thing from the constant stress of the horror he inflicted on me."

He sat silently for a long minute, his fingers tapping on my leg. "He'd wake me in the night suffocating me with my pillow, he'd hurt a puppy I loved and make me watch, shit like that. One day I'd finally had enough—he…he... I can't even say it, Penny, I'm sorry." Nate's words were barely above a hoarse whisper, the shame of his past still shrouding him. "He went too far—I decided to tell my parents or just kill myself."

Nate didn't speak again, and eventually I asked, "What did you do?"

"I told my parents about it. They hauled Kyle into the room, right in front of me, and asked him about it. Of course the perfect student, everyone's favorite relative, lied to them. And fuck, Penny, they believed that evil sack of shit! Over me, their own kid!"

"That I don't get—"

"Well, Kyle was cruel but he wasn't stupid. He'd made a game out of terrorizing me, and he'd set it up perfectly. Weeks before I approached my parents, he went to them with stories of how I was disturbed, saying all kinds of shit in my sleep, and making up crazy stories to *him* about how they abused me. So, when I sat across from them that day, to them it looked like what he'd said made sense. I didn't learn that part until years later when my mom told me. I was sent to a therapist, and Kyle continued to bully me for another month before he moved back in with his mother."

I shook my head, furious that the man I loved had to go through that.

"What happened to him? Please tell me he died in some horrific—"

"Nope. Reverend Kyle Curtis is married with four kids. He presides over the First Methodist Church in Wilson, North Carolina, our hometown."

"Holy shit. Did he change at least? Was what he did to you just the twisted, immature antics of a troubled teenager?"

"No, he's still a monster. His youngest daughter accused him of physical abuse four years ago—no one believed her. The good *Reverend* would never do such a thing. I actually went to the cops with her and her caseworker and told them my story—nothing ever happened. She eventually withdrew her claim—said she made it up."

"Did your parents ever believe you then?"

"Well, yes, I think so. After the abuse accusation, I talked to my mom about it, and she was so sorry, Pen. She just sobbed and sobbed. But my dad…he didn't want to hear about it—he said to leave the past in the past. It disgusts me."

I wrapped my arms around him—I wanted to shield him from pain.

"So, I buried that, or tried to. I always did drugs a little to numb things—in high school we smoked weed, did uppers, that sort of thing. In college I did X like most of the people I knew, but I was never addicted. Then, sometime after I made my first million from the software company I started, a girlfriend introduced me to cocaine. Do you remember Brandy Roberts?"

"Oh, shit yes, I hated that bitch. We were all so jealous that she snagged you!"

"Well, she snagged me alright. The more coke I did, the more I wanted. I could work for days on the stuff… Anyway, later, while here at the compound I started learning MMA type fighting from Dean, one of the security guys here that works the gate for extra money at night. It filled some empty space inside of me—I still crave drugs when I let my demons roam, but through fighting I've found a better release. And, it soothes the wrongs of the past to know that I can kick anyone's ass now, including guys twice my size like my fucked up Cousin Kyle."

"Thanks for sharing all of that with me." I kissed him on the cheek.

He leaned over and wiped the tears from my face. "I love you so much, Penny. You have no idea how much you've changed our lives. But, we have work to do. King Rex wants to see results when he gets back, and…he promised a reward if he likes what he sees." With a wink, he stood up and pulled me from the bench.

I followed him back to the center of the lawn, the mood lighter as he began to explain the Six Pillars of Krav Maga. Nate went easy on me, but I did fairly well that afternoon as he taught me how to defend myself. "We'll get you to the gym in the village to practice some as soon as you can be out in public again," he said as he handed me a towel.

Rex was back from his outing and watching from the bench; we'd staged an intense demonstration of what I'd learned for him. "No way! Not that shitty, stinky gym full of freaky folks," I said in response to his suggestion of fighting in town. Nate walked over and collapsed next to Rex as I dried off. "No, not there. There's a workout gym that does Krav Maga courses and training match-ups. It's run by Dean and his wife—safe and clean, I promise."

"You taught her well," Rex said to Nate, his hand floating down to rest on Nate's knee.

"Can I get a shower?" I was hot and sweaty from the afternoon's lesson.

Rex smiled at me as he stood from the bench.

"Yeah, and we'd love to join you, Princess," he winked, "but can you wait a few minutes? I promised a reward. To the kitchen," he said, gesturing for us to follow as he walked across the lawn toward the main house.

"Shit, it's melted." Rex was standing at the marble island in his kitchen, staring into a plain paper sack.

"You brought back ice cream?" I teased.

"Chocolate—the good stuff, too. Nate's favorite."

"Damn!" Nate walked up next to him and peered into the bag. "We can still make hot chocolate with it."

"In this heat?" I was a Vegas girl—we didn't do much hot chocolate where I was from.

"Colombian hot chocolate—chocolate caliente in Spanish—is the best in the world. We drink it year 'round," Nate explained, reaching into the bag and pulling out a bar of the mushy chocolate. "Add some cream and pure cane sugar to this, and it'll be killer," Nate said. "Did these bars come from the plantation?"

Rex nodded. "I brought it for you." Rex was crestfallen, his hand on Nate's back as Nate poked his index finger into the melted chocolate. "It's delicious anyway. I'm going to eat it like this." Rex poked his finger into the chocolate as Nate held it out to him, dipping in and sucking his long finger. "He makes the best chocolate—he sent beans too."

I cleared my throat—they'd forgotten about me.

"Princess feels ignored," Rex nudged Nate as they both looked at me. Rex walked over and took me in his arms. "I brought you something too—a bag of makeup, the good stuff. I forget what brand, but the local store ordered it from the States for me, it took a while but it's in your bathroom. Forgiven?" His nose nudged against my pouty face.

"Yes, but I didn't get any chocolate." I pressed against Rex, shooting Nate a flirty wink as he walked toward us, the chocolate in his hand.

"Well," Rex said, dipping his finger into the chocolate Nate held out, "I've *heard* that Nathaniel here doesn't mind sharing."

"Only with you two," Nate scolded, scooping up more of the softened chocolate and spreading it playfully across Rex's face.

I leaned in and licked the chocolate from Rex's cheek, his growing erection grinding against me as Nate pulled in closer. "Here's more," Nate teased, coating Rex's other cheek in chocolate. I moved in to lick Rex's other cheek, but paused at the last second. "Well, it's your chocolate…I think you should try it this way, it's delicious." Nate's eyes danced at the new game, looking to Rex for permission. "It's only fair," Rex said, moving his right cheek toward Nate.

Nate's eyes brimmed with lust as his tongue darted out, gingerly swiping across Rex's chocolate-streaked skin. "*Mm*," he moaned as his tongue stroked the cheek of the man he loved.

I reached up and unbuttoned Rex's shirt, pulling it open to reveal his hard, muscled chest. Rex's finger was still coated with the sticky chocolate, and with my hand around his, I slid the sweet candy across his left nipple. Without missing a beat, Nate lowered his worshipping tongue to lap at the chocolate on Rex's nipple.

Rex took the chocolate bar, still melted in the wrapper, from Nate's dangling left hand. Nate's now free hand wrapped around Rex's back, pulling their bodies close. As Nate licked his chest, Rex dipped his finger in the wrapper, and painted my lips with chocolate with the tip of his finger. Rex's lips fell on mine, our kiss deepening as our three bodies merged into a tangle of sweet, indulgent sensuality.

Later, naked and coated in chocolate, we made our way into the shower in Nate's bathroom. Both men lathered me up, their lips caressing me as four strong hands skated across my soapy skin. Once we were all chocolate-free, and horny as hell, Nate plunged into me from behind as Rex knelt down in front of me, his tireless tongue driving me to orgasm as Nate fucked me. When I couldn't take anymore, Rex leaned back against the marble shower wall, watching as Nate exploded into me.

Without thinking, Nate reached over to Rex's soapy cock and stroked it with his right hand. On my tiptoes, I reached up to kiss Rex as Nate's skilled fingers brought him to climax.

Chapter Ten

It was hot the next afternoon, and even though Rex's office was kept so cold I had to wear a sweatshirt, the thick air from outside seemed to permeate the stucco walls. I was clicking away on the travel software, preparing his next group of students for arrival, and Rex was at his large desk tapping away on his keyboard—with only his two index fingers. "How can you not type?" I said, the slow cadence of his hunting and pecking driving me insane. "I can type," he answered, never looking up from his keyboard, his glasses perched on the bridge of his nose. "With two fingers!" I shook my head and turned back to my own screen. "That's why I have you, Princess," he muttered as he finished what he was doing.

"Nate doesn't need my help with his stuff," I pouted, wishing I could be a part of both men's work lives.

"CEO Nathaniel Slater has an entire company of people to help him back in the States. My business is you and me, sweetheart."

"Well, boss, what are we doing this afternoon?"

"Hm," he mumbled, pulling off the glasses and tossing them on his desk, "I think I'm going to get some sun."

"Now you're talking," I said, already standing up from my desk chair. "I could use some color."

"No you don't. You can swim, but I want your perfect skin wearing sunblock."

"I live in Las Vegas, I can handle sun, it's…" I looked over to find him glaring at me. When he got like that, there was no arguing with him. King Rex had spoken.

"Yes, sir," I begrudgingly answered. "I'll swim, but can we get outside?"

"That we can," he said, standing up. "Let's go suit up."

"It's walled, let's skinny dip," I offered.

"I'd love to—but Maria is wandering around cleaning. She's a bit traditional."

I slipped into one of the slinky swimsuits in the drawer, picked out and stocked by Nate, and wandered out to meet Rex by the pool. Back home, I was self-conscious of my less than skinny body, but here I felt adored, beautiful. Nate was already out by the pool, parked in a chaise lounge, with a cold drink in his hand. "Hey, babe, that suit is rockin'," he gushed as he stood up and walked toward me. "Help me with this sunscreen? King Rex insisted," I said, rolling my eyes. "I happen to agree with him. I love your porcelain skin, and I love rubbing cream all over it," he winked. With a big glug of the lotion, he started rubbing it into my back in smooth, sexy circles.

I was nearly coated when Rex walked up and tossed a towel over his chair. "Do my backside?" Nate said over his shoulder to Rex, his lusty voice leaving no question that the innuendo was intentional. "Penny is right there, what the fuck?" Rex didn't seem to catch his obvious flirtation. Nate held up a bottle of oil toward Rex, "You're denying me an oiling up? Penny is slathered in sun block, this is tanning oil." Rex sighed and walked over toward Nate, his left hand reaching for the oil. "Turn around," he said gruffly. Nate grinned at me and winked. Before he could process what was happening, however, Rex had given him a hard push directly into the pool.

"So uncoordinated," Rex joked to me, rubbing the oil into his own chest. When Nate broke the surface of the water, he shook like a wet dog and glared at Rex. "That was rude, bro," Nate snapped, his middle finger in the air. "What ya gonna do about it, pretty boy?" Rex taunted. I walked over to my own chair, not thrilled that the sexy lotioning up had suddenly turned aggressive. "I think you might need to get wet," Nate smirked.

Rex sized him up before answering, "If you're man enough, get it done."

"Okay, enough, we're here to have fun," I said, eager to turn the afternoon back to friendly.

They ignored me. Nate pulled himself up from the pool, his rippled abs dripping water as his feet hit the pool deck. Rex didn't move, his powerful legs planted in a wide stance, the snug black swim trunks leaving little to my lusty imagination. Nate moved toward him, pissed off and determined to put Rex in the water. Nate came within feet of Rex, his navy blue trunks hanging from the V of his abs as he formulated his plan.

In a sudden rush, he caught Rex around the waist with both hands, his head butting directly into Rex's stomach, and both men toppled backward into the deep end. I stood up and ran to the side of the pool. I could see them underwater, Nate still had his arms around Rex, and they were twisting as Rex struggled to dislodge him. "Okay, this isn't funny anymore! Knock it off!" I yelled, as if they'd hear me that far underwater. They were twisting so much through the water I had no idea who was even on top.

I paced the side of the pool. I was an only child—I'd never seen two people I loved *physically* fighting. Sure, my parents yelled and screamed growing up, on the rare occasion when they were in the same room, but neither of them ever head-butted the other into a pool. A head finally broke the surface of the water—it was Rex's soaked down caramel blonde hair, which he shook from side to side. His large fist was wrapped in Nate's copper brown hair, holding him just below the surface of the water. I screamed and howled but Rex ignored me. With a slow underwater kick from Nate's foot to Rex's unprotected groin, Rex lost his grip on Nate as his body balled up in pain. "Fuck!" he screamed, his face twisted in an anguished growl as Nate emerged from the water.

"Stop it now!" I commanded again, my arms folded in front of my chest. Once again, they ignored me as if I didn't exist. Nate ducked under the water, this time of his own volition, and glided underwater to the far edge of the pool. Rex's head whipped toward him, and with a determined breaststroke he swam after Nate. In seconds, Nate was out of the pool and running with Rex close behind. "Don't run on the pool deck!" I yelled as if I were their nanny.

Nate made it to the grassy area to the left of the pool and turned around, his fingers curled, beckoning Rex to come closer. "Come get me, big boy, if you're man enough," Nate taunted. I grabbed my towel, slipped my feet in flip-flops, and scurried to the side of the grass. "Knock this off now," I sniffed, close to tears. "Oh, fight's on!" Rex roared, charging at Nate like a bull. Nate spun around, his foot catching Rex squarely in the face as Rex fell to the ground. Rex, his nose bleeding a dark maroon stream, caught Nate by the legs and yanked him down to the lawn before rolling on top of him.

Within a few seconds I was next to Rex, pulling him off the smaller Nate. "Stop it, you'll kill him!" Nate slithered from underneath Rex, and with a hard knock to Rex's ribs, pushed the bigger man to the grass. In seconds, Nate had Rex's large head locked down with his elbow around Rex's neck. Rex's fingers coiled around Nate's forearm, his strong arms pulling Nate's limbs from around his neck. In another flash, Nate was on top of Rex, his knees on Rex's chest, his hands fighting for position around Rex's neck. Rex's powerful legs rose up in an effort to kick the slender Nate back to the grass.

"Stop it, Rex, you'll hurt him!" I pleaded.

"Who the actual fuck do you think is winning here, Penny? Tell this asswipe!" Rex looked toward me, his expression instantly softer, the glimmer of play dancing in the corners of his midnight blue eyes. "What?" I couldn't manage to say much more, the men were frozen in front of me, as if I'd suddenly pressed the pause button. "Yeah, thanks for assuming he's going to win, Pen, appreciate it," Nate snapped, his lips in a hard line as he stared at me. "Oh, um…I just…Rex is bigger, like twice your weight…" I felt awkward being the center of their attention, despite the fact that I'd been screaming for the last ten minutes at them. "I'm not fucking *twice* as heavy as this dumbass, and I'm the one *bleeding* here, baby." Nate rolled off Rex, collapsing into the spongy lawn. "I won?" Nate looked quizzically toward Rex, who nodded. "You won, you wiry fuck. It's like wrestling a damn greased piglet—you're quick."

I sat down on the ground next to them and dabbed Rex's bleeding nose with my pool towel. "Good lesson for you, Princess. Size isn't everything," he winked. "Nate can out fight me any day of the week—because he's fast and he's smart. He always knows his next move, whereas I was flailing—reacting rather than strategizing. That's why Nate here is the one teaching you the hand-to-hand stuff and not me." Nate rubbed my leg, his body cradled by the soft grass, his lips turned in a satisfied grin. "I just wanted to roll around half naked with him," he teased with a wink. Rex rolled the towel and snapped it playfully at

Nate. "I thought you were really fighting," I explained, still shaken up. "Sorry, babe, just oversized boys releasing pent up testosterone. We didn't mean to upset you," Nate said, his hand still caressing my leg.

That evening after dinner, I rounded the corner to where the men were relaxing in the corner garden. I usually referred to this part of the grounds as "the smoking section" because it was where they often smoked cigars after dinner. Both men sipped bourbon, looked at the stars, and talked about life. I sometimes joined them, sipping a glass of wine, while other times I enjoyed soaking in the hot tub instead. Tonight, I finished my soak and decided to bring them out a fresh bottle from the liquor cabinet. Coming around the wall, I paused as I heard them say my name. They were deep in conversation, and I didn't want to intrude.

"Yeah, things are different with Penny here now—I agree. I'm not saying no, Nate, I'm just saying—give me time. I don't know—this is all uncharted territory for me."

"I know—and I love what we have. I don't want to fuck it up by asking for more. But...I can't pretend like I don't feel what I feel, either."

"I don't want you to. We've always talked about everything—I don't want that to change. To answer your question," I heard Rex gulp audibly, followed by the clink of his glass being set down on the metal table, "with Penny there, yeah, I'm more comfortable physically and could probably allow a little more. There, I said it." Nate chuckled and said,

"Lightning did not strike." Rex laughed and said, "The ground did not swallow me up."

I stood in the shadows, absorbing the pieces of their conversation and trying to make sense of it. I jumped when Nate came around the corner and nearly ran into me. Embarrassed and guilty, I held the bottle of bourbon out to him. "I-I didn't mean to listen. I was bringing you guys a fresh bottle." Nate smiled, taking me into his arms. "We don't have anything to say that you can't hear. I need to pee—go sit with Rex, I'll be back in a minute."

I emerged from the shadows where I'd been hiding.

Rex smiled warmly and patted his lap, "Come sit with me—we missed you."

Rex took the bottle from me as I crawled into his lap. "Johnnie Walker Blue Label, not too shabby of a choice," he said, opening the bottle and pouring the amber libation into his tumbler and Nate's empty glass on the table. "Taste it," he said holding it up to my lips. I sniffed the contents of his tumbler—it smelled sweet, syrupy. "This one is smooth—smoother than that cabernet you were sipping on earlier." I took a cautious sip, then another, less cautious one. "It's good," I had to admit. "More kick than I'm used to, but yeah—I can see the appeal."

"You smell like smoke," I whined, handing him back his glass and nuzzling into his chest. "An unfortunate side effect of puffing cigars, I'm afraid." He was quiet, sipping his bourbon and pouring another. "Nate wants..." He trailed off, as if the words escaped him. "More touching?" He exhaled and pulled me closer. "Yeah—well, he didn't say it exactly like that."

"I heard some of it. From what I know about him, he mostly just wants to be able to show you how he feels, even if just a little."

"I know and I get that. I've gotten comfortable with small displays of affection—that was hard for me at first. I touch Nate in ways I would never touch another dude. And, I want him to be happy. It's just never gotten…sexual."

"He respects your boundaries, how you feel. I know I do."

"Thanks, Princess. I'm not proud of this—but I'll just admit it. The idea of being touched by *Nate* doesn't bug me. The idea of being touched by a *guy* does, though. What does that say about me?"

"It says you're a normal conflicted person who is honest about his feelings. Don't feel guilty—we all have our limits. And…it also says you're able to take an honest look at it."

He took a deep breath and slowly let it out. "This whole thing with Nate threw me for a loop. It was like there was some tear in the fabric of my universe that allowed him to slip in to my heart. I couldn't make sense of it—until you came. Now, it all just clicks—the three of us are like three broken circles that somehow fused to make a perfectly bonded whole. It's all there, and I'm happy with it—but I want for Nate to get what he needs, too."

"So what are you going to do?"

"I'm going to drink a whole shitload more bourbon and then I'm going to take you both to bed."

"Oh," was all I could say. I didn't want Rex to go further than he was comfortable with, but the idea of my two men getting more intimate did turn me on.

"What if everything fizzles the second he…" Rex sighed and took another big swig from his glass. "It'll hurt him."

"I won't let that happen. I'll be there—focus on me."

"That's never hard to do, sweetheart. You set me on fire every damn time."

Hours later, the normally in-control Rex was slurring his words and stripping his clothes off in the yard. By the time we got him to Nate's bedroom, he was naked. I pushed him into the sofa in Nate's room, falling on top of him. I'd never seen Rex even close to drunk. He loved to sip his whiskey, but he wasn't one to ever get sloppy—he was too much of a control freak. "Kiss me, Penny," he howled, pulling my face to his. We made out slowly, my tongue savoring the syrupy-sweet zing of the whiskey on his breath. I sensed Nate moving around the room, but kept my focus on Rex. I wanted him ready to explode by the time I urged Nate to touch him.

The lights dimmed and the door locked, Nate stood over us. Rex pulled my mouth from his, pushing my face toward Nate's. "Kiss," he said, "I wanna watch." Rex's erection ground against me as my tongue found Nate's. Our mouths never parted as Rex yanked roughly at my clothes in a desperate attempt to strip me. Nate's agile fingers assisted him, and within minutes I was naked, my bare legs straddling Rex's wide hips. Nate's hands reached under my breasts, kneading them as he kissed me. Rex was insane with need—his hips bucking as his desperate cock sought my pussy.

"You're torturing me!" His whiskey-laden breath was at my ear, his fingers trying to pull me from Nate's kiss. I slid my lips from Nate's and looked down at Rex. Tonight, for the first time, I wanted control. Both men were waffling with a big decision— a calculated, choreographed attempt at *more*. I, however, wanted to end the thinking and just become three people driven by insatiable, label-less, boundary-less passion for each other.

I pushed Rex back, purring, "You said you wanted to watch, big guy. You want to see Nate fuck me?" His hips rose up again as he hissed, "Yes!" Nate's agile fingers found my nipples, giving them a harsh twist before pulling me up from Rex's naked body. "On your knees, Penny," Nate said, his voice rich with desire. I knelt on the floor in front of the sofa Rex was flopped across, his large hand slowly stroking his swollen cock. My eyes never left Rex's as Nate stripped off his own clothes and positioned the head of his long cock at the soaked entrance of my pussy. "*Ah,*" I moaned as Nate entered me. The force of his thrusts caused my large breasts to sway from side to side, taunting Rex as he watched us fuck.

I wasn't sure how much longer the inebriated Rex would be subdued into just watching, so I pushed back against Nate, meeting each thrust with a push of my hips onto him. "I want to watch you come, both of you," Rex groaned, his own thick cock glistened at the tip. Nate's hand reached around to stroke my clit as he fucked me, the clenching of my pussy against his throbbing cock milking him to an explosion deep inside me.

When I recovered from the force of my own climax, I crawled toward Rex with Nate still pulsing inside me. My tongue sought his heavy balls, teasing them as I licked up and down. "You're killing me," Rex groaned, his hands wrapped around the back of my head. "You want to come in my mouth?" I teased, flicking the barbell piercing on the underside of his cock. "Yes," he groaned. "Can Nathaniel help?" I asked, nervous I was pushing him too far. "*Yes, just…please…*"

Nate slid out of me and crawled up in front of the sofa, hovering over Rex's hardness as I massaged Rex's shaft with my tongue. I licked up and down Rex's length, toying with the metal pierced into his shaft, purposefully keeping him on the edge. I wanted to tease him to the point that he'd explode with pleasure when Nate's tongue decided to join in. Rex's eyes closed as his legs braced—he couldn't take much more. I nodded to Nate—he licked his lips, but hesitated. I wasn't sure he'd go through with it, but in a sudden rush of sexual energy, his lips wrapped around the head of Rex's cock, Nate's cheeks hollowing as he sucked far too hard. *Clearly he's never given head before*, I couldn't help but think to myself.

Rex groaned, a half grunt, half growl, as Nate's mouth pulled at him. My fingers found the seam rising from Rex's hard sac, stroking as Nate found a rhythm, loosening his suction for an up an down motion. I let my own hungry tongue slide underneath Rex, and as I poked his salty skin, I felt the tension of his shuddering orgasm. By the time I looked up, I expected to find Nate's mouth away from the ejaculating Rex, but instead he held on, sucking every drop of Rex's seed into his worshipping mouth.

Rex was asleep when I leaned into Nate and asked, "Are you okay?" I knew Rex wasn't the only one who would struggle from the new type of intimacy. "Yeah," he smiled, licking his lips. "That was…different!" He laughed as we fell together. "Let's get him into bed—have you ever dealt with a King Rex sized hangover before?" He shook his head as he pulled Rex up and leaned him over his shoulders, "Never."

We slept that night as usual, intertwined limbs in a giant bed, tossing and turning in a perfect loving unison as the sun forced its way back to the sky.

Chapter Eleven

I sat across from Nate in the large living room the next afternoon. I'd been working on Rex's financials all morning long. Nate was right—Rex had plenty of money, but it wasn't managed well and there was too much cash slipping through his fingers each month. When he asked me that morning to take a look at his numbers, I was honored. He trusted me, and more importantly, had confidence that I had the brainpower to help him out.

After lunch, however, I needed a break from staring at spreadsheets and bank statements, so I challenged Nate to a game of chess. His phone rang as my bishop moved in to check his queen, but he glanced at the screen and ignored it. "Ladies?" I joked. He laughed, his eyes glued to the chessboard. "None that could beat me at chess—you are smart as hell, Penny. Your father was an idiot to not put your brainpower to work. Nah, the call was from my dad. I don't know why he bothers."

"What if it's an emergency?"

"Then he'll leave a message or call Rex. In fact, he'll probably call Rex anyway."

"What does he…I mean, what does your dad think your relationship with Rex is exactly?"

He shrugged, his long fingers caressing his rook. "I don't really care. Besides, I'm not sure I know myself."

He placed the rook down and removed his fingers, leaning back in his leather wingchair in defeat.

"Checkmate. One more game?" He nodded and began to set up the board as Rex walked in, his expression grim. "Yeah, Al, I will—uh, no, I'll work it out somehow. Take care of yourself." Rex clicked the button to end the call on his phone and looked to Nate.

"How the fuck is *daddy*?" Nate asked through gritted teeth. "What does he want? Money?"

"No, man, uh…It's your mother. Her cancer is back. They don't—"

"What?" Nate stood up, his arms crossed in front of his chest. "She's in remission, she's going to be *fine*…" I stood up from my own chair and wrapped my arms around Nate's waist—he was shaking. "Nathaniel, this time it's serious. We need to get there ASAP."

Nate shook his head, raking his hands through his wavy coppery brown hair. "This is just a ploy dad is using to get me to…" He sat back down into the chair, pulling me into his lap.

"I'm sorry, Nate, this time—he said she's as sick as he's ever seen her, and she's calling for you and your sister."

"Holy shit." Nate wrapped his arms around me, squeezing so tightly I struggled to breathe.

"We'll leave in a few hours. She's at a hospital in Wilson. I think we can manage to fly in without attracting too much attention."

"Wilson? They left her in the tiny fucking town's hospital? Why didn't they move her to Duke?"

"I don't know. Let me have them get the plane ready to fly us into North Carolina."

"I won't leave Penny alone, it's too dangerous," Nate squeezed me even tighter.

I couldn't speak. I lost my own mother, whom I adored, not more than a couple of years ago to heart disease.

"No, we're not letting our girl out of our sight. I'll whip up some fake paperwork. It wouldn't pass the TSA, but it'll look good enough for a local agent without the means or incentive to really check."

I sat on Nate's lap stunned. I was going back to the States. "Penny, go pack. Grab a suitcase out of my closet." I nodded to Rex before leaning in to kiss Nate before he gave me a quick pat on the back to go. In my room, tossing clothes into one of Rex's suitcases, the tears flowed down my cheeks. Rex wasn't one to get excited over too much, but I knew him well enough to know that he was shaken, afraid for Nate.

"Hey Princess," Rex said, walking in to my room and sitting in the chair in the corner. "It's a big deal, isn't it?" He glanced at the door before answering, "Yeah, sweetheart, she doesn't have long left. We have to be there for him—he's going to be battling all sorts of emotions. We can't let him self-blame, or worse, relapse into addiction. Pick out a couple of conservative black dresses—I'll hang them in the plane with our suits."

My heart ached for Nate. This was the first time I'd been in love, and I never imagined the pain of watching someone you love hurt. "His dad isn't a bad guy, is he?"

Rex shook his head, "No, he's made some missteps, but who hasn't? Nate wants someone to blame—he wants a villain to point the finger at. I'd give anything to have had a father like Al Slater instead of the sack of shit dickwad I spent my first ten years with."

"Is he alive? Your father?"

"No, baby, he's long since dead. Both of them—self-absorbed trash. Social Services took me when I was twelve—mother dearest died in a bar brawl a few months later."

"Oh my God, that's horrible." I'd lived a privileged life, and despite not feeling loved by my father, I couldn't imagine the trauma Rex suffered as a young child. "Were you adopted?"

"No, Penny, no one adopts twelve year old boys, and the State of New York makes a terrible parent. I bounced from foster home to foster home, some not bad, most horrific, until Evelyn noticed me in high school one afternoon." He smiled at the memory. "We were in biology class—I was a good student. I knew it was my only chance to climb out of the shithole of my life. Evelyn, though..." He chuckled as he said, "She was a cute cheerleader, popular, but more interested in having a good time than studying. She was stuck during a lab and leaned over to me. 'Roger, it's Roger, right?' she said. 'Can you help me? I'll take you out for a burger after school if you do…' And from then on, much to the shock of the entire town, we were a couple. I ended up staying with her family the last two years of high school. No one ever loved me before Evelyn."

The tears rushed up again—my heart broke for the two men I loved dearly. I wrapped my arms around him as he buried his face into my hair. "I love you, more than anything." His large hand wrapped around the back of my neck, pulling me closer. "I love you too, Princess. You have no idea how much I need you."

"Nate loves you, too."

He nodded into my hair, nuzzled there to hide the emotion I knew he felt. "After she left me, she said she never loved me. That sent me into a self-destructive spiral."

"People just say that stuff, she didn't mean it."

"I don't know whether she did or not, but the idea of never being loved by *anyone* just broke me apart. I had good friends—you forge a strong bond with men you fight for your life with, but the kind of love…No, I never had it. Until Nate."

I was anxious to hear how the relationship between the men had evolved into more than friendship, but Rex pulled back from my hair and leaned back. "That's too long of a story for now, Princess. We really need to get going."

"You'll tell me though…?"

"Yeah, baby, I will. I'll tell you all of it, and I'll pray that you'll still love me when my demons are dragged from the closet."

The flight to North Carolina took forever. Normally, I'd have whined, but instead I sat by Nate's side, holding his hand as we watched a comedy on the iPad—neither of us laughed. Rex, however, leaned back in one of the oversized leather chairs and slept. He could sleep anywhere, no matter what the circumstances around him. We made two fuel stops, and both times Rex nervously rushed out to greet the airport staff. At both stops, a customs agent boarded the plane. My heart lurched as the second agent spent more time, closely looking from me to the fake passport Rex made, but he nodded and smiled to us. "Welcome home," he said as he stamped my fake passport, complete with several fake stamps detailing my entries and exits from South America. "I need to look in the cargo hold—just a formality, you know—coming from Colombia and all." Rex nodded to the man, "Don't I know it. Worked DEA shit for fifteen years."

We were quickly cleared on our way, and we all breathed a sigh of relief. "We're going to have to get your paperwork, babe. Is it in your penthouse?" I looked to Nate with a smile—I was happy anytime they reminded me that my life with them was permanent. "My passport and birth certificate are, yeah. What else do I need?"

Rex sat down across from us and fastened his seatbelt. "That'll do for now—but once you're out of danger, we'll need to get you a visa."

"And I'm sure daddy is worried…" Nate shot Rex an uncomfortable glance.

Early the next morning, we checked into two rooms at a semi-decent hotel close to the hospital in Nate's hometown. Nate joked he got two rooms instead of three to keep them guessing who the couple was. We collapsed into a king sized bed in one of the rooms, fully clothed, and slept until the alarm went off.

As soon as we could, we headed to the hospital the next morning. Rex and I waited in the long, sterile hallway in plastic chairs as Nate hugged his sister and, much to our relief, his father. "I'm sorry, Dad, I-I didn't know," he said with tears floating in his steel-blue eyes. "You're here son, that means the world to me. She wants to see you." The three of them walked into the hospital room arm in arm.

I waited with Rex for over an hour. He rejected my offer to go get everyone coffee with a gruff, "You don't leave my sight. Not even to take a shit, got it?"

"Romantic," I replied with an eye roll.

"We took a huge risk leaving the compound with you. If anything happened to you…" He took a deep breath and walked to the windows at the end of the hall.

Nate's mother, Nancy, continued to decline over the course of the week. The family sat by her side night and day, praying, begging, and pleading with God to save her. On Thursday afternoon, she died in her sleep at the young age of fifty-six. Nate was inconsolable as we held him in the chapel of the hospital, four loving arms wrapped around his tall, lean frame as he wept.

We managed to get him to eat only a few crackers that night before we went to sleep. The viewing was scheduled for the next afternoon, and the funeral the day after. I begged to be allowed to go, but both men insisted that I stay behind with Rex— there was too great a chance of pictures of me leaking out, putting all of us in danger. The media was already arriving to the small town and setting up news vans outside the hospital. The return of missing billionaire Nathaniel Slater wasn't going to go unnoticed.

As was our routine, we went to bed curled up in front of the television, only this time, rather than me in the middle, Rex spooned up behind Nate and we both held him tight as he worked through the grief of losing a parent. While I dozed off to sleep with heavy eyelids, I heard Nate whisper to Rex, "Say it." Rex moved toward him, but I kept my eyes shut to give them some space. "You know I do," Rex's deep voice said. "I need to hear it tonight, please." Nate sounded broken, pained. "I love you, Nathaniel, you belong to me, forever."

When I woke the next morning, the hot sun streaming through a crack in the vinyl curtain liner, I looked over to the men I loved. Nate's head was on Rex's sleeping chest, the same way I normally slept with Rex, and Rex's strong, comforting arms were wrapped around Nate's back, holding him close. I crept to the coffee machine as they slept, flipping through the muted TV channels. A local morning show was running the story of Nate's return from the Amazon to be by his mother's side as she bravely fought cervical cancer.

I wasn't allowed to be seen at the funeral home, but Nate's father, Al, invited us for dinner at their house after the viewing. I wore the simpler of the two black dresses I'd brought, and as I slipped into the shiny black pumps, I asked Rex, "So when they ask, who am I with?" He was standing at the mirror, carefully tying his black silk tie into a Windsor knot. I was so used to seeing Rex dressed for jungle survival that the sight of him in a suit peaked my libido, but I fought the urge to flirt as I remembered the pain Nate was in.

"Well," he said, straightening the tie and adjusting his collar, "that's up to Nate, I think. Al has hinted a few times that we might be *together*, but he's never come right out and asked. I'm sure the addition of you really has them scratching their heads."

"How *would* you define it?"

"I wouldn't," he said flatly.

"Well, I mean, you two don't have sex—I mean not together, not together alone, anyway. But Nate would if…"

"Can we move on?" He slid his designer jacket on over his broad shoulders and grabbed a black pair of socks from his suitcase. When not in combat boots, Rex rarely wore socks. He often wandered the house shoeless, and I loved his sexy bare feet. He was ink-free from the waist down, and the contrast of his untouched skin below with the elaborate tattooing above was stunning. I hadn't found any further body jewelry on Rex, and I'd explored every inch of his fine physique, but he did have several piercings that he left open—ears, the other nipple, and a few more man-made holes riddled his gigantic ballsack. In addition to the holes, his body was lined with thin, barely visible scars in straight lines. He also had a puffy, larger scar from what appeared to be a surgery underneath where the word *Trust* was inked below his ribs. My mind drifted back to what to refer to their sort of bi, sort of not, unique relationship.

"I'd say you are hetero life partners," I eventually decided as I swiped a line of black eyeliner around my eyes.

Rex dropped his sock, his head whipping around to glare at me. "What the *fuck* does that mean?"

"I think it's from *SNL*…"

He sighed and finished pulling up his socks before sliding his feet into a stiff pair of leather shoes. "I haven't seen *Saturday Night Live* in sixteen years, baby girl."

"You should wear underwear," I teased as I dabbed lip-gloss around my mouth. Rex was usually commando, but I didn't want his metal piercings showing through the satiny fabric of the suit at a family dinner. "I'm not a teenager, Penny, I'm wearing underwear, see?" He pulled the waistband of his trousers down to show me the band of his brand-new Calvins.

"Okay, let's go, I hate to be late. We're supposed to meet the family back at the house," he nagged as he looped the battered Omega watch he wore over his wide wrist. With metal and ink covered by the dark suit, he looked more like a successful businessman than the primal Rex I was used to. "I hope all this grief is over with soon, Princess, because I can't wait to fuck you again. Or watch Nate fuck you…"

"You're a voyeur," I teased, slipping gold hoops into my earlobes.

"Oh big time. Watch, be watched—yeah, baby, that's *definitely* my kink. But if anyone other than Nate ever touches *you*," he made a cutting motion across his throat with his hand.

"What about Nate with someone else?" The thought of it made me cringe with jealousy, but I was curious about the depth of Rex's kink. "So curious today, baby girl. Before seeing *you* on the plane that night, I was never interested in watching Nate with anyone else, no."

"He said he'd been with women in Colombia. Did that make you jealous?"

"Hm," he mused, his index finger stroking his chin. "I guess I didn't really think about it at the time. But now, you both belong to me, we belong to each other. We are three, and it's what's right for us. I don't need to have it labeled as anything."

"You know, Nate's not here… I could kneel down and…" I dropped to my knees in front of him and licked my lips. He looked down at me, his caramel color hair flopping down over his forehead. "You're a naughty girl, *and* trying to make us late. But, it's been forever, and I'm about to burst looking at your ass wiggling around in that dress."

"You went two years without sex, right? What's a few days?" I teased.

"I went two years without sex with others, I jacked off all fucking day."

"So is that a yes?"

"Open up but be quick, and I'll try not to ruin those glossy lips."

"You're so fucking bossy," I teased as I unzipped his suit pants and worked his hardening cock out through the fly.

"Watch your fucking language, Princess, or I'll turn you over my knee again right now." I wrapped my lips around him, my tongue toying with the titanium barbell along the underside of his growing cock. "*Fuck, baby, you're good at that*," he groaned, his legs bracing as I sucked him slowly into a shuddering orgasm.

The tip of my tongue flicked around the head of his cock, greedily cleaning every last drop from him. "That's enough, we need to go," he said, slipping his half-erect cock back into his pants. "What about me?" I wiggled my hips—I was so turned on I'd come from the slightest touch. He reached down and pulled me to my feet. "No time, sweetheart, you'll have to wait." With a swat to my ass, he directed me to the door. "No fair," I pouted. He looped his arm through mine and walked me into the open elevator. "Life is *not* fair, baby."

Chapter Twelve

After the funeral, the plane was loaded up with our American supply bounty as we strapped in our seatbelts for the flight back home. *Home, it was now home to me.* Nate was still dressed in the black suit he'd worn to bury his mother. We'd given him space to just be silent and grieve, so little had been said after we picked him up for the airport.

Within an hour, Rex was asleep in his chair. I looked over to Nate—I had no idea what to say. "Come back and just lie with me?" His steel blue eyes looked so sad as he stood from his chair and reached a hand out toward me. I walked with him to the back—the bedroom where I first woke up after being drugged and taken by him. It seemed like forever ago—then I was terrified, now I realized that these two men risked their lives to save mine.

He pulled off his suit coat and tossed it over a side chair, followed by his black tie. We curled up together against the padded headboard, my head on his chest as he held me against his crisp cotton dress shirt. "I'll get makeup on your shirt," I said absently. "I don't care," he muttered, his long fingers running through my hair. "Does it ever stop hurting?" I nuzzled closer into him and honestly answered, "No. But it gets easier to deal with as time passes. You'll never stop missing her."

"I feel so guilty for not being there more. If only I'd—"

"You can't change the past. She knew you loved her, that you were doing the best you could."

"She said that to me—that she wanted me to be happy and healthy. She was so proud that I'd been clean for so long. I just keep seeing her there, all hooked up to tubes and wires, in so much pain." His eyes misted with tears as I held him. "Tell me something about her, something that will always make you smile."

He smiled a little. "She always cut the crusts off my sandwiches. I mean always—even as a grown man. One time I told her, 'Ma, you don't have to do that, I eat crusts now.' She said, 'Nathaniel, it's our special thing.' I loved her so much."

"Love, not past tense. Love doesn't die, just bodies."

"I like that, Penny. Did I tell you that my dad plans to come out to Colombia next month? He says he wants to learn some jungle stuff, but I don't see him doing that."

"I'm glad your mother brought you back together. He didn't ask about *us*, though?"

"He did," he said quietly, his lips brushing across my forehead. "And I told him the truth. He was a bit surprised, but echoed my mom. He said as long as I'm happy, he's supportive."

"Your sister?"

"She wasn't happy at all. Didn't you see her flirting with Rex?"

"Oh my God no!" I giggled.

"Talk about awkward…" We laughed, and as we did I felt him relax, the emotional drain of the last week relenting for a few stolen moments.

"I've missed touching you, Pen. Feeling your skin, hearing you moan—the way you say my name when you come. I-I'm ready to feel again."

I turned my face to his. "I love you, Nate," I said before kissing him—the kind of kiss that binds you in a moment so perfect, so complete it lives forever. His hand stroked my cheek as his tongue explored my willing mouth. It had been so long since we'd made love, and I needed him desperately. His hand ran up my back before reaching around to pull the sweatshirt over my head. I clawed at his shirt, opening it to reveal his chiseled chest. I planted a row of kisses across his toned pecs before focusing on his hardening pink nipples.

"*Shit, babe, I've missed you,*" he moaned as I stroked him through the suit pants. Within seconds, we'd undressed, our skin craving the intimate contact of two lovers parted for too long. I straddled his hips, gasping as he entered me in one long stroke. "*Ah,*" I nearly screamed as his long cock knocked against my sensitive cervix. His hands held on to my hips, raising me up again. "More?" I slammed down on him again, taking his entire length as I moaned, "*Yes!*"

With his thumb stroking my swollen clit, I continued to fuck him hard, up and down, all in one solid stroke, over and over until I shook from the force of my climax. "*Fuck, when you do that, it makes me come, too,*" he grunted, spilling into me as his hands dug into my hips. I collapsed on top of him, my head against his shoulder, panting as I tried to catch my breath. When I moved to pull off him, his hands grabbed my hips once again, holding me in place. His tireless cock stirred inside of me as he said, "We're not done yet—there's still lots of catching up to do, babe." My Energizer Bunny of sex went non-stop through three climaxes, never once withdrawing from my soaked, throbbing pussy. I lost count of how many times I came that night on the airplane before we finally rolled into the covers in exhaustion.

"You can go *forever*," I said with a shake of my head.

"Ah, King Rex has his moves, but he can't do *that*."

From the door, his voice boomed as we startled. "*Please*, boy, when I was your age, I'd have fucked her until she couldn't stand up, fucked you, fucked my hand, fucked the wine bottle, fucked the sink, and that would have just been foreplay. Then, I'd be ready to fuck the—"

"We get it," Nate said with mock exasperation.

"You were spying on us," I said lustily as Rex walked over to the bed. "Don't flatter yourselves. You woke me up with all that moaning and groaning. Sounded like two cats in heat." He slid in behind me, fully dressed against my sore, naked body.

"You left me with sore sloppy seconds?" Rex teased with a gentle swat on my bare ass. "Sorry," Nate said with a grin and a shrug of his shoulders. Rex pulled close to me in a classic lovers' spoon. "How are you feeling, man? No urge to—"

"No," Nate interrupted. "Not once did I want to turn to drugs. I had you two there to get me through."

"I'm beyond happy to hear that. You're on your way to being free of it."

We were quiet in the dimly lit airplane cabin, cuddled up together in the wide bed. I thought Nate was asleep—his eyes were closed. "He looks peaceful," I whispered, rolling over to face Rex. "Yeah, I was worried this would send him into a tailspin. I'm super proud of him."

"Would you ever get a tattoo for Nate?" Rex's tattoos were a constant source of curiosity for me.

"He has one," Nate yawned behind me, rolling over to wrap his arm around my waist. "There's a Nate in there?" I'd spent far too much time pouring over Rex's ink, but had never seen the word *Nate* etched into his body. Rex took my hand and placed it on his left side, the hard ripple of his abs underneath my probing fingers. "*Trust*, that was for Nate. He's the first person I ever truly trusted."

"It's over a scar…" My finger ran over the faint puffy line beneath the script of the word *Trust*.

Rex sighed and looked at Nate—I'd touched upon something.

"It's okay, you don't have to tell me." I meant it—as curious as I was, I didn't want to push Rex.

Nate was silent, waiting to see if Rex would share. "I have an addiction too, Princess." His words hung in the night as I absorbed them. "To what?" I finally asked. "Pain. I use physical pain to mask emotional pain. I'm a cutter, or I *was* a cutter. This," he ran my finger over the scar again, "is the last time I purposefully cut myself with a blade."

My heart hurt for him. *All the fine, faint scars on his perfect golden skin...* "All the piercings—I did those, to myself, to numb some emotion or another." I lay there silently, my fingertips still tracing the scars along his torso. It was no longer a mystery why the three of us were drawn together—we all shared some vein of self-destructive behavior, we all drove those we loved, who loved us, away. My fingers drifted to his pierced nipple, the one that still contained a titanium barbell through it. "That mother fucker," he said with a nervous laugh, "hurt more than anything I've ever done. I've taken some serious pain, but a needle through that nipple nearly caused me to pass out. This one wasn't so bad." He pointed to the empty left nipple piercing. "The dick piercings were tiny pinpricks *on* my prick compared to *that* bitch." I was silent, absorbing his words, struggling to understand.

"Did it ease the pain?" I finally asked.

"Of course not," he answered softly. "It never does. Just like drugs didn't ease Nate's pain, just numbed it. Taking endless douchebags to bed sure as hell didn't make you feel better, did it?" I didn't answer—he was right. "So the night she told me she'd *never* loved me and that our son's death was my fault, I spiraled. She'd left me months ago, and had already filed for divorce. In a drunken moment of weakness, I called her and she said those words to me and hung up. I locked my bedroom door—Nate was already living with me at the time—and pulled out a new razor and began to cut. This time, though, it wasn't enough. The blood and the faint sting didn't ease the pain, so I pulled out a field knife, wiped it with alcohol, and cut a nice, satisfying slit across my side— right where you feel the scar." Nate rustled behind me, the memory difficult for him.

"Well, I fucked up somehow—I'm an emergency doc, not a surgeon, and was drunk off my ass. It wouldn't stop bleeding and I passed out on my floor."

"Oh my God."

"Nate somehow…"

"I *sensed* it, Penny, I *felt* it. I was sound asleep, but jolted up in bed and knew I had to get to Rex. He doesn't believe it, but it happened."

"Like divine providence," I offered.

"I don't believe in *that* shit, but I'm grateful as fuck that he broke the door down."

"You're a Catholic, how can you not accept a miracle?"

"I hedge my bets, that's all. A little insurance, but I never said I *believed* it. Anyway, he got to me—he stopped the bleeding."

"He'd given me his crash-combat med course just a few days prior," Nate explained.

"After I came to, he even stitched me up—he did a pretty decent job with those soft keyboard hands," Rex joked.

"You gave him *stitches*?" I turned to look at Nate.

"At his direction, it was terrifying."

"I would have done it myself, but I'd had way too much to drink. My hands were shaky," Rex added matter-of-factly.

"Anyway, I came clean that night about the cutting, and we talked all night long. I told him things I've never said to *anybody*."

"So you were able to stop the…the cutting?"

"Pretty boy made me promise, but we made a deal. No more cocaine for him, no more cutting for me."

"I broke that deal once—fell off the wagon. But that seemed to be it, I haven't had the urge since, but I'm careful," Nate said as his lips brushed against the back of my neck.

"I love you both *so much*," was all I could manage to say.

Nate was dozing off behind me, exhausted from the night and emotionally drained. Rex pulled me close and said, "We both love you, Penny. You're the final piece of the puzzle. We need you."

"Sounds like more divine providence," I said with a smile.

"You're pushing it, Princess," Rex growled, pulling me into him with a sleepy yawn.

Chapter Thirteen

Back in Colombia, life resumed at its normal pace as I hung in limbo—someone was still trying to kill me but, nestled into life with these two men, I managed to ignore the threat and spent my time settling into life with the two men I loved. Nate mourned his mother, but day by day got stronger.

Late one night the week after we returned, I was on the bed, hovering over Nate on all fours—his tongue flicking at my swollen clit, my own lips wrapping around the engorged head of his cock. Rex was behind me, standing next to the bed where Nate and I engaged in our indulgent 69, his thick cock toying with the tight entrance to my pussy until I begged him to fuck me. "*Needy girl,*" Rex moaned as he sunk into me, "*one man's not enough?*" My tongue found Nate's cock once again, teasing it in long, languid strokes. "*Are you going to come, sweet Penny?*" Rex pulled out of me, then plunged to the depths of my throbbing pussy in one solid stroke. I grunted, "*Yes...fuck!*" I was on the brink of orgasm, about to cascade over to the point of no return when Rex pulled his cock out of me. Before I crested, Nate's tongue left my clit—his warm breath torturing my pulsating bundle of nerves.

I sucked harder at Nate, desperate for him to pleasure me—I was so close to the edge of ecstasy. Nate's mouth was moving beneath me, but not on my hungry pussy. His lips were wrapped around Rex, inches from me yet so far out of my reach. "*Can you taste her sweetness all over my cock?*" Rex grunted at Nate, who moaned in response, the sound of his tongue savoring my arousal from Rex so erotic, so perfect that I never wanted it to end—even though my own empty tightness yearned for them.

"Lick my balls clean, then you can have more cock," Rex scolded, playfully pulling himself from Nate's mouth to lay his heavy balls across Nate's open mouth. Nate's cock twitched and his own balls tightened as I toyed with his shaft. Being able to touch Rex, to pleasure him in such an intimate way was heaven for Nate, and I was thrilled that I was able to facilitate contact between the two men I loved. Rex would never allow that level of contact with just the two of them alone, but with me there, in the middle, he was comfortable with Nate's touch.

Rex slid his long cock into Nate's mouth, fucking his throat as Nate swallowed the punishing cock with a gurgle. Without warning, Rex's hand yanked his cock from Nate's worshipping mouth and impaled me with it, my tightness opening to take all of him. The sensation of Nate's tongue on my clit while

Rex fucked me hard from behind was more than I could take—I shook from the force of my climax as Nate pushed his hips into me—fucking my mouth as my throat strained to hold him. His salty ejaculate filled my mouth as he pulsed beneath me, Rex's cock never letting up, pounding me from behind, his hands clenched around my hips as he fucked me. When Rex came inside me, Nate's tongue rose up, dipping around Rex's still throbbing cock, buried in me, to lick up as much of Rex's come as he could—the combination of the two people he loved mingling on his tongue in a complete erotic synergy.

Chapter Fourteen

I was blissfully asleep in Nate's loving arms when it happened. Rex was in the jungle, and Nate and I had spent the evening sipping chilled white wine and tossing back popcorn as we streamed episode after episode of *Californication*. We had delicious tipsy sex, and collapsed together in his comfy bed.

It happened so fast, I thought it was a dream—or a nightmare. I heard Nate scream, then a loud thud. My eyes couldn't focus in the dark, and I struggled to understand as I screamed for him—and then everything went black. When I came to, I was in a room—a bedroom. My head throbbed—I'd been hit with something, but after that an electric shock had knocked me out. I felt the burn marks on the back of my neck from the device. Nate wasn't with me, and I prayed that he was okay.

I was tied to a bed—my feet by ropes, my wrists taped together with silver duct tape in a dark room. I was still too weak from the blow to stay conscious, and despite the urgent voice in my head screaming for me to escape, I drifted back into a pained sleep thinking of Nate.

"Who the *fuck* are you?" My eyes fluttered opened as they strained to focus on the man standing in front of me. The room was dark, and my head still throbbed. "Uh," my eyes blinked as he became clearer. His English was impeccable, but there was a faint trace of a South American accent laced in. He wore a silvery suit—his black hair was longish, silky but slicked back, his face covered by a well-trimmed dark beard. A large gold hoop ran through one ear—he was handsome, exotic looking.

I couldn't think of a decent lie, so I settled on the truth. "Penelope Sedgewick," I answered. "Oh fuck!" he screamed in recognition, not at me but toward the hallway behind him. I strained to sit up. He looked down the hall and shouted, "Woman, get the fuck in here, *now!*" He walked over to me, shaking his head. "*That loco bitch…*" he muttered, reaching down to raise me to a sitting position, my bound wrists going numb as they rested on my lap.

"Sir, she's not here, Mr. Pablo." A young American appeared in the doorway, he couldn't have been more than a teenager.

"Why did she bring this woman to my house?" He spat each word in anger.

The teenager shook his head. "I didn't know until it was done. I'm sorry, I've tried to watch the Mistress. She plans to turn the captive over to Murdock in the morning—he's coming in from Vegas to pick her up. I guess he's been paid to…well, he was looking for the blonde in the States."

"That lunatic is going to let her sick hatred draw that crazy **DEA** fuck and his buddies *right* to my damn doorstep!" Pablo's words were angry, but underneath, they were laced with fear.

"What should I do, sir?"

"Listen, Derek, I have a meeting late tonight, an important meeting. I'll be home before dawn and I'll decide then. Keep a close eye on the Mistress— don't let her do *anything* to dig this situation any deeper."

"Yes, sir," Derek answered as Pablo slammed the door.

"Um, Derek is it? You're American too?" I slathered on my flirtiest voice.

"I-I'm from Utah."

"It's pretty there. I was raised in Nevada, do you think—"

"Enough! It's not working on me, lady."

"No, I just…I have to pee. I don't want to soil the bed, could you…?"

"Oh," he said, blushing a scarlet red, his eyes drifting to my bound ankles. "I-I need to ask, I'll be right back."

I felt it was time to put my fighting skills to the test when Derek came back. He was small, and far from confident. The idea of fighting scared me, but Nate had trained me well and the thought of being turned over to some thug who was hired to kill me was far more frightening.

I looked at my wrists—Nate had spent a few hours the week prior going over how to get out of the common restraint, and I was good at it. But, our lessons always involved standing. I hadn't done it from a sitting position. With all the concentration I could muster, I raised both bound wrists as far as I could over my head. In a quick wave of bravado, I forced my arms down and out as hard as I could, mentally reminding myself to break through any perceived resistance. The first try I failed—I let hesitation and doubt get in the way. The second time, however, as my elbows cleared my hips to each side, the tape broke away with a sharp tear to my skin. I sighed a breath of relief, regretting all the whining I'd done about the bruises and strain of learning how to escape restraints. *Those lessons, hopefully, just might save my life*, I thought as I formed a plan.

I looked to my feet, struggling to untie the ropes that bound me. I strained to hear Derek coming back, but there was nothing. I was able to get one foot undone, but as I started the second one, the door flung open. *Shit! I was so close!*

"I've got you, Princess," his deep voice cooed as he burst into the room and worked to untie my other foot. "We've got to go," Rex urged. I wrapped my arms around his neck as he lifted my numb limbs from the bed.

As I rubbed my wrists, I looked over and saw her standing in the doorway. She was lit from the dim hall light behind her. Shiny, jet-black hair hung across her cheek in an oblique bobbed cut. Her pale gray eyes shone against her ivory skin. At her side she held a handgun, gripped tightly in her fist. The gun quivered slightly back and forth as her hand shook.

"Roger, your time has come. Go join our son…" She raised the shiny black pistol with two hands in front of her. Her hands were wobbly as she leveled the gun at Rex. He didn't go for his own weapon holstered in the waistband of his jeans. I didn't think she was bluffing, so I reached for it—but his large hand stopped me.

Rex's calm voice spoke as he pulled me behind him.

"Evelyn, put that down…you don't even know how to use that thing," Rex smirked. Evelyn's eyes stayed coldly locked on Rex's as she grasped the slide of the pistol and charged it, the metallic clink echoing off the polished wood floor.

"Evie, you won't shoot me; you can't. We both know it." Rex was cool as ice even when staring down the barrel of a handgun. "Look at you, hand shaking like a leaf just holding that thing. Do you even know how to use it?" Evelyn just stared at Rex coldly and nodded her head.

"You know me well enough to know that this isn't the first time I've had a gun pointed at me, and the last guys who did it *actually knew what they were doing* with one. Put that away. I'm taking Penelope here home, that's all." He reached for my hand, pulling me behind him as he took a step toward the door.

I heard the horrid *BANG* and felt the hot muzzle flash before I fully realized what happened. One step in front of me, Rex suddenly stumbled, then fell to the ground. My ears were ringing from the intensity of the sound of the gunshot, but I heard the *tink-tink-tink* of the expended brass shell casing bouncing off the ground. I fell to my knees beside Rex on the wooden floor. He lay on his side, a red circle on his shoulder just beginning to ooze red where the bullet hit him.

Evelyn stood motionless, handgun still held out in front of her and a thin cloud of smoke from the gunshot rising in the air next to her. "You fucking shot him!" I screamed at the soulless bitch who just threatened to take away the man I loved. Without thinking, I yanked Rex's gun from his jeans. Before I could fire, she shot again, directly into Rex's abdomen.

As she turned her pistol to me, I trained Rex's Glock 19 handgun on the woman. Time seemed to slow down as I aimed at Evelyn, keeping my eyes open and picking out the white dot of the front sight, the dark outline of her body just behind it. I squeezed the trigger and the long pull of it with my finger seemed to take forever. Just as Rex had taught me, the shot caught me by surprise, the gun jumping back in my hands and the sound of the shot painfully stabbing my eardrums.

Her body crumpled over and she fell hard onto the wooden floor, her eyes never closing, in the red pool of blood slowly creeping from her body. The pistol clattered across the floor and her body spasmed in a horrific final fury. I sat there stunned for a moment, my ears ringing and the sharp ammonia-like smell of the gun smoke stinging my nose. I laid down the Glock and moved to Rex—his face was white; sweat covered his forehead. He didn't speak, instead he grunted and gasped shallowly for air. The shoulder wound had blood slowly oozing from it, but Rex was holding his gut, where the more serious wound was, his shirt beginning to turn red in a bloody halo around his hands. I dug into the backpack he'd dropped on the floor and pulled out his combat first-aid kit. In seconds, I'd pulled his shirt loose and stuffed the hole in his gut with the clotting pad—the blood slowed but continued to flow from his mid-section. With my right hand, I pressed on the wound, so hard he groaned and moved to dislodge my hand, as my left pulled out the pressure bandage. I opened it with my teeth—not sanitary, but I didn't have any more hands. Rex's eyes were closed, his eyelids fluttering and various muscles in his body twitching erratically, randomly. "Penny," he whispered, his face to the ceiling. I struggled to apply as much pressure as I could as I dressed the wound. "I love you, Penny, always," he said, his voice a hoarse whisper. "Tell Nate—I love him, too—like he wanted me to...I do, I swear."

"Tell him yourself," I snapped, continuing to frantically try to stop the blood running from the gunshot, my eyes drifting in terror to his shoulder, where a large bloodstain had formed on his shirt around the ragged hole through the fabric.

How am I going to get him out of here? I looked around. I guessed I couldn't just call 911 like at home...

The heavy door burst open, a dark bearded man held a rifle in front of him with a flashlight attached to the front—it had a curved magazine like the AK-47 Rex had taught me to shoot. He was dressed in jeans and a black t-shirt, and had sleeved tattoos on muscular arms like Rex. He paused as he swept his rifle-mounted light across us in the dimly-lit room. *Fuck, one of Pablo's goons!* I knew my handgun was no match for his rifle. The thug surveyed Rex and I on the floor, and Evelyn's dead body close by. The man squatted at Evelyn, removing his glove to feel for a pulse at her neck while keeping his rifle trained on me. Rex's head turned toward the door at the sound, his eyes opening wide and following the man as he stood by Evelyn's limp body. Rex recognized the shadowy man.

"Dan, is she gone?" Rex asked the man, his voice barely above a whisper. The man nodded as he rushed over to Rex. "She's gone," he confirmed, his eyes settling on Rex's wounds. "*Fuck, Colonel...*Okay, stay calm. Her?" He pointed to me. "With me," Rex coughed out. "Nate is in the basement," Rex choked out, "save him first." Dan nodded, answering, "They already have him, he's safe—broken arm, maybe, not much else. They're on their way with the truck—you're going to be okay, buddy." Dan inspected the shoulder with his flashlight then moved down to look at my work on the abdomen wound.

Rex grew whiter, weaker. I never let up on the pressure on his wound, but my heart was racing. He gasped for air, only able to take small, panting breaths and coughing up sinewy spatters of blood when he exhaled. "Bro," he whispered to Dan, "I think...I'm...done, man." Rex raised his hand and grasped the man's forearm. "Gimme...Last Rites."

I shook my head. "You aren't fucking dying on me!"

"Such language," Rex coughed, scolding me, his voice so low I could barely hear him.

"You don't need that, it doesn't look that bad to me, dude."

Rex stared at Dan, wheezing. "I can't move my legs," he paused to cough, "I think it's my spine." Rex's eyes rolled up and back and he closed them, his whole body relaxing.

"I don't think so, man, don't you fucking give up on me," the man gently slapped Rex's cheek and he opened his eyes again.

"Do it, Dan. This is it. I'm serious." I continued to hold pressure on the wound, realizing my own hands were soaked in Rex's blood. I couldn't believe what was happening, what I was hearing.

Dan leaned over and pulled a silk scarf from a pocket.

Rex smiled, coughed again, and took as deep a breath as he could. "Forgive me Father, for I have sinned," Rex began, his voice fading, as the unlikely priest knelt beside him.

"He's not going to die!" I screamed, praying to wake up from this nightmare.

He faded toward the end of the Last Rites sacrament being preformed by Dan, or Father Dan I guess would be more appropriate of a title. I wasn't able to rouse him, despite my blubbering and begging. Father Dan calmly continued his duties, fulfilling Rex's last request of him. I, however, wasn't interested in the saving of his soul for the afterlife. I wanted him to wake up—I wasn't about to let him leave me.

"Please, I love you so much, wake up," I begged, never letting my hand leave the bloody wound in his gut. He was breathing—and I clung to that. "They're here, hang on to him honey, okay?" Dan said as he walked to the window, pulling the sash from around his neck and tucking it back into his pocket. I nodded, praying for help and soon. Gunshots rang out, and Dan ran to the door with his rifle aimed down the hallway. The house was silent as heavy boots marched up the stairs—I didn't know if the good guys or the bad guys were upon us. "Yeah, yeah, hurry, he's in here—he's been hit...bad," Dan said to a man coming through the door. Three more men filed in behind him, all in body armor and carrying rifles just like Dan's.

"Okay, get Colonel Renton to the hospital— yeah, the big one in Bogotá, Chaplain Bowen and the chick there can stay with him," the first guy said to others. "We'll handle the rest," he said, nodding to Dan. "You got Nate out?" I asked looking to the armored man. "Yes, they already got him out—I think they took him to the same hospital we're taking Colonel Renton to." I sighed a small breath of relief. "Don't let go of that wound until a doctor gets to him okay? I'll stay with you two," Dan said. Three of the men came over to lift Rex's body, and despite their assurances that they could care for his wound, I refused to let go and ended up walking next to Rex all the way down to a large armored van parked in front of the sprawling mansion.

Dan came in and sat across from me right before the van began to move. He pulled water from a compartment in the wall and offered me a bottle, but I shook my head. I was parched beyond belief, but didn't want to let go of Rex's wound. Dan stood up and walked over next to where Rex was lying across the bench seat in the rear of the van. He reached up and flicked an overhead light on before examining Rex's shoulder injury. "This one has stopped bleeding, it's not going to be worrisome. But, honey, that abdominal shot was…" I grimaced, "I don't care, he's not dying!" Dan nodded and shot me a look of pity. "I'm Penny," I added. "Are there medical supplies here? Should I rewrap the wound?"

He took a deep breath and let it out. "No, I wouldn't. We're not far from the hospital. I think you have the blood completely stopped—keep doing what you're doing, Penny." I looked down at my hand—he was right, the blood flow had stopped. "I've known Rex for a very long time," Dan said as he sat back down on the seat across from me. "We…I haven't known him long but—he's everything to me. He can't die—I love him too much," I said, fighting the tears that threatened to fall. "He's a good man—I'm honored to have worked with him. I can't believe Evelyn shot him," he exhaled as he looked down at the floor. "Penny, listen, I'm going to tell you something important—Rex would want me to. Don't say *anything* about what happened tonight—not a word. I doubt they'll question you—the local authorities—but if they do, you don't remember anything after you were taken." I nodded, the legal implications of the fact that I'd shot someone slowly dawning on me.

The van slowed to a stop, and two of our rescuers slid the heavy door open. A gurney was raised into the van, followed by several Spanish speakers in medical uniforms. They spoke to me, but I didn't move my hand as they lifted Rex onto the gurney. "Penny, you have to let go—they've got him now," Dan's soothing voice said in my ear. His hand was on top of mine, gently urging me to release Rex. I let him pull my hand off, and was relieved that blood didn't flow from the wound. "Can I stay with him?" I begged the medics taking Rex into the hospital as I jogged next to them. "No, we're taking him into surgery. Please wait in the family waiting room," answered a nurse in perfect English. "Thank you," I muttered as they wheeled him into a swinging door, Dan pulling me by the arm to keep me from trying to follow. I was terrified I'd never see Rex alive again as I crumpled against Dan.

We sat waiting for what seemed like forever until one of the body armored men poked his head in the waiting room. "I'm sorry, Major Bowen, we need to get you back..." He glanced over at me apologetically. Dan gathered his few things and stood up from the plastic chair. "I'm sorry, Penny, they don't want me hanging around a public place for long. I have to go." He grasped my hand one more time and said, "I'll be praying for Rex, and for you. I'm sure we'll meet again some day." As quickly as they'd come, the Americans were gone. I was left alone in the stark waiting room with fluorescent flickering lights and a vending machine that I had no money to use.

Two hours later, the English speaking nurse came in and pulled her mask down. "Is he okay?" I stood up nervously, waiting for her reply. "He's alive," she began, "and seems to be doing fairly well in surgery. The bullet is close to his spine, so the surgeons are being very careful." I exhaled in relief. "Oh thank God," I said. "How much longer?" She glanced back toward the door she'd come in from. "I can't say, Miss. I need to get some information from you. The people who brought you two to the hospital seem to have disappeared. Are you his next of kin?" She pulled a small pad of paper from her pocket, and unlatched a pen from a chain around her neck. "I-I… No, I'm his girlfriend. I live with him, and our…friend Nate is here, too. He was brought in with a broken arm earlier I think." She nodded and jotted a few things down before asking, "Your name?" I paused— I wasn't sure if I was still in danger, or how to answer, so I settled on the truth. "Penelope Sedgewick." She wrote the information down and looked up from her pad. "I'll check on your friend. Nate?"

"Yes, Nathaniel Slater. They said he broke his arm."

"Oh, well, they probably wouldn't have kept him for a broken bone. I'll see what I can find out." She turned and left as I slumped into the hard plastic chair. It'd been forever since I'd eaten or had anything to drink, and the injuries from my capture were throbbing. I stood and the room spun for a few moments before I felt well enough to explore the main hospital in search of a water fountain. However, as I walked toward the door, a doctor in scrubs entered the waiting room. "How is Rex?" I blurted out. He shot me a confused glance, and raised his hands in a questioning gesture. *He doesn't speak English, great*, I thought. The man gestured for me to sit, so I sat back down in the plastic chair.

"I don't know who Rex is...the man you're here with has identification that he's Roger Renton?" I nodded excitedly, "Yeah, Roger. How is he?" The doctor pulled a plastic chair in front of me and sat down. "Miss, he's very strong and pulled through surgery better than expected. However, the bullet that I removed from his torso was quite close to his spine. He will live, but he may not walk again. We won't know until he comes to and begins to heal. I'm sorry." My heart pounded and I was sure I was going to be sick. I remembered Rex telling Dan that he couldn't feel his legs... *At least he's alive*, I reassured myself. "Can I see him?" The doctor stood. "Yes, you can sit with him. He probably won't be awake for several more hours, though."

It took another half an hour for them to lead me in to a regular hospital room where Rex was lying in a bed hooked up to machines and devices. Even in a pale blue hospital gown, his skin ashen and a beeping machine monitoring his vitals, I could feel the strength emanating from Rex. I sat down in a comfortable chair next to his bed and reached for his hand. "I love you—keep fighting," I whispered in his ear.

I dozed off in the chair, never letting go of his hand. "Miss Sedgewick?" I was awakened by a dark haired man with a local accent walking into the room. He wore a light blue suit—ill fitting and cheap looking. He was clearly not cartel—I'd been around long enough to realize they dressed to the nines. "Yes?" I answered. "I'm Second Sergeant Marco Reyes with the Colombian National Police. I just have a few speedy questions about the occurrence last night?" I stared at him—his English was choppy, the words not quite smooth as if he had to give a lot of thought to what he was saying. "Do I need to have an attorney present?" I asked. "Americans," he said under his breath. "You must tell me what you recollect about what you perceived with your vision last night?" *Perceived with my vision? This guy clearly learned English from some book.* "Well, I was taken from my boyfriend's house with some sort of zap and a blow to the head. After that, I don't remember anything." The man nodded, as if he expected that to be my answer. "It is the same thing your friend spoke to me." As the police officer said the word *friend* Rex squeezed my hand. I instinctively looked over at him—he was still unconscious.

"Friend? Nate's here?" The man nodded and looked up from his notes. "It is true. I spoke to Nathaniel Slater before arriving to this room."

"In the hospital?" The man stared at me as if I were being obtuse.

"Affirmative, Miss. The man you speak of is in a room in the T section."

"What is the T section?"

"Head trauma," he answered slowly. He stood to leave, reaching into his pocket and producing a business card. "If you should happen to remember, you may call me if you feel. Otherwise, I bid you good day." In a flash, the man was gone.

"*Mother fuck*, I hope I handled that right…" I said aloud.

"You shouldn't swear in a fucking hospital, baby, certainly not around your comatose *boyfriend*." *Oh my God, he's awake!*

"Rex!" His eyelids fluttered open. "You handled that fine. That douchebag doesn't give a shit what happened—he wants to clear it off his busy schedule. If the local police really wanted to be involved in that mess, they wouldn't have sent a low-ranking, barely English speaking beat detective over to ask questions." He looked around the room before asking with a smirk, "I'm your *boyfriend*?"

"What did you want me to call you?"

"I can think of a lot of titles I'd like to be to you, Princess. Boyfriend just sounded high-school, that's all."

I exhaled, relieved he was awake and speaking to me. "How do you feel?" I asked, my fingertips flitting over his cheek. "I've been better," he chuckled. "What was that shit about Nate? Head trauma?"

"I haven't been able to see him, but your peeps said it was only a broken arm."

"My *peeps*," he repeated, making fun of me. At least he was acting like my Rex.

"I'll go find Nate. But Rex," I thought about what the doctor had said… *Was he paralyzed?*

He looked over at me, waiting. "The doctor said… The bullet was near your spine. After you were shot you couldn't feel your legs. He said that you might not be able to…" I couldn't finish. I choked back tears as he took my hand again.

"Penny—I'm not going to be paralyzed."

"I-I know, it's just… I'm afraid."

"Sweetheart, look," he said, gesturing toward his feet. They were moving.

"Oh thank God." I felt a wave of relief wash over me.

"Loss of blood, pressure on the spinal cord—that caused the numbness. Luckily for me I got a surgeon with decent hands. My gut feels like a truck drove over it, but I can move just fine. Hand me my chart, Princess."

"What?" He pointed to the end of his bed where an old-school metal covered clipboard with a stack of papers hung. "It's not like the States…they are still keeping paper patient charts."

I glanced at the chart, but argued, "Um, I don't think you're allowed to mess with that, they…"

"Give me my damn chart, baby girl."

I handed it to him, my eyes on the door. I was a rule follower type, and Rex for sure was not. He flipped through the pages as I waited impatiently, eventually closing it and pointing to a hanging plastic bag at the end of the bed. "Is that my shit?" I looked over at the black plastic bag. "Oh… I don't know…" I replaced the chart and looked through the plastic bag—Rex's bloody clothes, his wallet, belt, shoes, and a small zipper bag of his jewelry floated around the bag. "What did the chart say?" I finally asked. He shrugged, "Nothing major. They got both bullets out, no apparent nerve damage, release as soon as I'm stable." I didn't believe him—the night prior I thought he was about to die, and now he made it sound fairly routine. "Maybe I'll read it myself," I argued. "It's in Spanish, but knock yourself out," he teased.

"I'm just worried, Rex. I mean, last night I was holding your insides in with my hand!"

His face softened. "I know, baby, I'm sorry. There's nothing bad in the chart, I swear, but the wound is major. It's going to take a long time to heal."

We sat in silence for a long time until he asked, "Hey, is my wedding ring in there?"

"Seriously?" I snapped.

He looked confused. "What? I've worn that ring for over twenty years, it's special to me."

"The ring from a woman who tried to kill you!"

"Penny, I'm tired. Can we argue about this later? Will you please go check on Nate? And be careful. If anything happened to either of you, I *would* die. I love you—more than anything or anyone."

"It's hard to be mad at you when you say stuff like that," I said, kissing him before heading toward the door.

"Tell the nurses I'm awake on your way out. I'm sure they'll want to poke me with needles."

Chapter Fifteen

"I murdered her. I killed your ex-wife!" I was inconsolable, the guilt enveloping me. Rex had been in the hospital several days—and he wouldn't allow me to leave, so I slept in the empty bed next to him each night. The security staff from the compound brought me a suitcase with clothes, but I was going stir crazy in the hospital day after day. Nate was being held while they evaluated the bump on his head, but each day brought a new promise that he'd be released at any moment. Until then, Rex made a sizable donation to the hospital to ensure I'd be allowed to stay under his direct supervision.

After lunch that day, the weight of what I'd done—of shooting another human being—crashed down on me. I was inconsolable, becoming more and more upset as I relived the night in my head.

"Penelope! Stop it," he snapped, reaching down to grasp his aching wound as he stilled. In a calmer voice, he said, "You didn't *murder* anyone. She tried to kill me, and then went for you—you defended yourself *and* me, there's nothing else you could do. You did well. *I* fucked up—I let arrogance and over-confidence cloud my judgment and it almost got both of us killed. But you—you saved my life, Penny."

"You really didn't think she'd do it?"

"No, I let past feelings interfere with my instincts. The Evelyn I loved was dead long ago. I guess she really didn't ever love me."

"Oh, she loved you Rex! She never stopped."

He thought for a second and asked, "What makes you say that?"

"The passion—underneath that drug-addicted zombie façade, there was a woman scorned who would rather see you dead than not with her. The thing is—she wanted you the way she wanted you, not the way you are."

He thought for a moment. "Not the way I am *now*. I changed a lot once I started doing the special ops shit—it was hard to go back to helping with the dishes and going out to a movie after all that. We grew so far apart, the path back was just too convoluted. It's sad all around."

"Do you ever want to have kids? Or was losing one just too hard?" I couldn't help but ask; the question haunted me as I thought of Noah, his dead infant.

"Sure, I'd love to have babies. You feeling like breeding an army of mini Rexes and Nates?" It was nice to see him teasing me again. I smiled and answered, "Someday, I'd be honored to. But not yet!"

"It's a deal, Princess."

We sat in silence. I thought he'd dozed off to sleep when he asked, "How is Nate? Is it really just a broken bone, or is everyone bullshitting me?"

"It's a broken arm, his left luckily. He has a bump on the head they want to evaluate, but other than that, he seems okay."

"Why haven't I been able to see him then?"

"Uh, he's…I really don't know. I think he feels like he let you down because I was taken. But, there's no way he could have stopped those goons."

"He needs to let that shit go. We all know he'd die for you. Is he letting them treat the pain?"

"No," I answered honestly.

"Stubborn ass," Rex shook his head in irritation, but his face betrayed a proud glow. Nate denying opiates showed his commitment to recovery from drug addiction.

"You heal better when pain is managed," he said. "Have them give him this," he added as he reached for a paper and pen from the bedside table. "It won't trigger his addiction, but it'll give him just enough pain relief that he won't go reaching for something stronger."

I took the paper—it looked like a prescription, scribbled and confusing.

"They don't already know that?" I asked, not meaning to question him.

"No, Penny—this isn't exactly The Mayo Clinic. They try, but…just take the paper to his doc, okay?" I nodded and headed for the door. "And I want to see him—*now*," he commanded. "Uh huh," I answered, knowing full well that Nate would have to be dragged to see Rex.

"But why?" I whined as I sat beside Nate's bed. His arm was in a cast, but other than that he looked good.

"I was supposed to protect you, and I failed miserably—yet *again*."

"He's anxious to see you, Nate—in a good way. I think it hurts him that you haven't been to see him."

"No, he has you."

"Stop that shit—it sounds like jealousy talking, and we're beyond that. Get up and come with me or I'm wheeling your ass down there." I stood up and walked to the door, ready to commandeer a wheelchair if needed. No way my two men were staying apart for one more minute.

With a stubborn sigh, Nate stood and pulled his hospital gown around him. "They're letting me go this afternoon, might as well face the Colonel now," he said. We walked across the long hospital to Rex's room—Nate was silent, like a death row inmate being lead to imminent slaughter.

Rex smiled as Nate shuffled into his room. I squeezed Nate's hand—more than a part of me was worried that Rex's calm had been false. I held my breath as we approached Rex. He looked up at Nate and his expression warmed, and I knew we were going to be okay.

"Hey, man," Rex said, reaching a hand to Nate. "How's the arm?"

Nate froze—his face morphing into a ghostly white. He dropped my hand and flung himself at

Rex's side, kneeling on the floor by his bed. "Holy shit—you're hooked up to all this, it's all my fault…"

"It's not," Rex answered calmly, his fingers reaching over to run through Nate's hair in an intimate gesture that had become their own.

"You told me to protect her…I put you in danger, I put…" Nate's body shook as his mind went through the could-have-beens.

"You did what you could do. Evelyn paid off Maria to let those thugs into my house. Into *our* house."

"The maid?" I couldn't believe she'd been responsible. He nodded, "Yeah, she did this with Rodrigo's help."

"Why would he…?"

"She's been fucking him forever. And, Evelyn hired her. Plus, that amount of money set her entire family up for life, most likely."

"So it wasn't because of me? Because of the drugs?" Nate relaxed, the weight of guilt lifted from him. But his calm quickly turned to anger. "What are you going to do to them?" Nate asked, his face red in rage.

"Nothing. I mean, they're *fired*, of course. But, they aren't the real villains here."

Rex's fingers went down to Nate's face, his thumb cradling the indent of Nate's elegant chin. "There's nothing you could do, okay?" Nate nodded, his eyes rimmed red as he fought the swell of emotion.

We sat there silently, Nate on his knees on the floor beside Rex's hospital bed.

"Seeing you like this…" Nate whispered.

"I'm going to be fine, man, I swear. We trained the Princess well." He smiled at me, reaching a hand out for me to come closer.

I crouched on the floor next to Nate. Like two baby chicks waiting to be fed by a momma bird, we waited for Rex's guidance. He held up his hand, three fingers splayed out at us. "Three," he said, "we are three. I love you both."

I reached up three fingers and held them to Rex's, my hand tiny against his. "Three, I love you both," I repeated.

Nate flushed, a warm glow lighting his face. He held up three fingers from his left hand to ours and repeated the words that would become an oath binding us together.

"Now, *take* those meds the doc is going to give you. Trust me, they won't trigger anything. When they release you, get a room at the hotel across the street. Don't let Penny out of your sight—she's been stuck sleeping here this whole time. I think it'll be another few days before I can convince this quack to let me go home."

"I will," Nate nodded, his confidence restored.

"She *should* be safe—Murdock, the guy hired to do the hit on her, has been, well, *taken care of*. Evelyn was going to turn Penny over to him as soon as he got back—apparently he was on his way from Vegas where he was looking for her."

"So what's Pablo's role in this?"

"None. He wasn't involved. But, thanks to Evelyn's lunacy, there was a massive DEA raid on his mansion. It just *happened* to turn up two kidnapped Americans. It's a shame that Major Daniel Bowen, a special ops Chaplain, had no choice but to shoot Evelyn with my Glock in self defense." He winked at us and added, "Helps to have friends you can call in a favor to." My mind drifted to the night of our rescue, and the burly Priest, Father Dan, who saved our lives. "Poor drug lord Pablo, his wife is dead and he's sitting in a Colombian jail cell. DEA turned up all sorts of incriminating shit in his tacky mansion."

"Won't Lynn just hire someone else to do the job?" Nate shot a worried glance toward me.

"Oh, that piece of shit. Well, as *odd as it may seem*, he was involved in a hit and run accident the other night on the Strip. Seems he didn't make it," Rex shook his head in mock sadness. Clearly his network of contacts ran deep.

"I'm safe then? Can I call my dad?" I was relieved to finally not have a price on my head.

"I think you're safe, yeah, but can you just wait until we're all home? I'd feel better then."

"The rooster wants all of his chickens home to roost before he can relax," Nate teased.

"What the fuck do you know about livestock, Mr. Internet Billionaire?" He shot Nate a smile. "Go back and rest, take those meds, and get yourself released so Penny can get out of this hospital."

"Yes, sir," Nate quipped with a mock salute. He kissed me before heading back to his room.

"You're so bossy," I said to Rex with a grin.

"Damn straight I am," he pointed his large index finger at me. "Now, park yourself over on that spare bed and let me sleep so I can get the fuck out of here."

Chapter Sixteen

I sat on the floor in the hallway outside of Rex's room a few days later, my knees to my chest, my head resting on them, exhausted. Nate had been released, and I spent my nights across the street at a hotel with him, but my worry for Rex prevented me from sleeping. After sitting with Rex all morning, I'd left the men to go down the hall to get a candy bar from the vending machine, and when I returned, Nate and Rex were embroiled in conversation. I drifted off, but at some point Rex's deep voice lulled me from sleep.

"No way—no. Nate, I won't lose you...*we* won't lose you. Forget it."

"I-I don't want to. I just thought that you might want to be with Penny, that the two of you could be a regular couple, be... You know, get married, have kids." Nate's voice was ragged with pain. I knew he loved me, loved us both, so much that he would sacrifice himself for our happiness. My heart ached for him.

Rex's answered, low and comforting. "Do you love her?"

"Yes, more than anything. Both of you... But how can this work? Seriously? The *three* of us?"

"You brought us together, and it's right. I don't give a rat's ass about what anyone thinks about anything—I never have. I don't get the impression she gives a fuck about *traditional* either. Did you even ask her?" Rex's tone was loving, but he was annoyed.

"No, I wanted to see...I'd do anything for you two to be happy."

"We are happy, bro. Did you seriously think she'd be okay without you? Nate, it'd be like asking her to cut out half of her heart." In a lower voice, Rex added, "And...half of *my* heart. No fucking way."

I was ecstatic that Rex wanted the three of us together and rejected Nate's offer to step aside. It *had* crossed my mind more than once in moments of doubt that I'd be asked to choose between these two men—to love only one of them. When my mother was dying, my father asked me to choose him over her. The idea of it was sickening—I loved them both. To him, though, my decision to stay by her side was a betrayal. I *never* wanted to be forced to choose between people I loved again. My love was complete with both men, and I prayed that they could accept that. As I wiped away a tear, I knew that Rex understood.

The room was silent, and I rose up to rejoin them when I heard Rex speak.

"Is it enough for you?"

"From her? Of course! I want her to love you."

"I meant from me? I'm never going to give you the level of… I doubt I'm ever going to give you what you desire from me. Is what the three of us have, physically, enough?"

"What we have is enough—with Penny, it's complete. You two are my all; I just…I don't want to ever hurt her. What if I fuck up again?"

"Then you fuck up again, and *we* are here for you this time."

A doctor came up behind me, urging me forward in agitated Spanish I didn't understand. "Inside," he barked when I didn't move. I walked into Rex's room through the open door. He was propped up on pillows, his golden color once again gracing his skin. Nate's long fingers rested on Rex's forearm. He didn't remove them when the doctor came in behind me, and Rex, to my surprise, didn't either.

Rex smiled at me and tapped the edge of the bed. "Come sit, Penny—seems the doc here has news."

The doctor spoke in loud, hurried Spanish— the news sounded dire, except when he was finished speaking, Rex smiled. "Gracias," he said as the doctor left. "What?" Nate asked nervously. "I can go home tomorrow."

Nate was thrilled; I wasn't. "No, it's too dangerous, who will take care of you?"

"We will," Nate answered, annoyed that I wasn't as excited at the news as he was.

"Yeah, of course, but I mean shouldn't we hire a nurse or something? I don't want to risk his health with—"

"With us idiots?" Nate snapped.

"I didn't mean it like that. I'm just afraid, that's all. I thought we lost him not that long ago."

"Penny, I'm a doctor. I can care for these two wounds myself. My legs are fine—I need to rest, recover, keep the pain at bay." I nodded, the idea of going home beginning to sink in. "This arm will be in a sling for a little while longer until the shoulder wound heals, so I'll need you two, but we can handle this." In a whisper, he added, "Home is far safer, and cleaner, than this place."

"I'm going to go get the house ready for Rex—we need groceries, supplies, and bourbon," Nate said, reaching for my hand and pulling me to my feet in front of him. "Will you stay here with him tonight? I don't want him left alone." I nodded as I wrapped my arms around his waist. His fingers raised my chin to look into his mesmerizing eyes. "I love you, babe. Call me if anything changes, okay?" He leaned down to kiss me before sliding his fingers through Rex's hair. "Thanks, man," Rex said as Nate left the room.

I sat on the bed next to Rex, careful not to put pressure on his injuries. "Penny, you're going to have to help with the meds. Nate can't be around the kind of shit I'm going to be on—it has to stay locked in the medical room. Under no circumstances do you let Nate have access to that area, are we clear?"

"Yes, sir," I answered to the domineering Rex. I knew, and Nate knew, he shouldn't be around prescription strength painkillers.

"And do *not* let him give me a sponge bath!" I giggled as he took my hand in his. "Nate wanted to leave us—let us be a regular couple," Rex said with a grimace.

"I overheard from the hallway. I worry that he doesn't know how much I love him. How do I ever show you both that my love is equal, that—"

"Love isn't a finite quantity, sweetheart," he interrupted. "Our love, the *three* of us, is threefold because we share it—multiplied not divided. Our way may not work for everybody, shit it wouldn't work for most people, but for us, it just is. It's *right* and perfect. Nate got off-track in trying to fit us square pegs into round holes, that's all."

"I love you both so much," I said as his hand wrapped around mine.

With a sigh, Rex explained, "He wants us happy—but I need him in the equation to be happy. I don't feel like I'm sharing either of you. The three of us together, however that shakes out, is what I want. Maybe if I'd met you first, I wouldn't see it that way. But, honestly—I wouldn't have let you in if Nate hadn't already broken down that barrier. Without him, I never would have allowed myself to love you."

"We just need to get back home, together," I answered.

The next day, we piled into the large, overly-chilled van, driven by one of the security guards rather than the fired Rodrigo, and took Rex home.

He was his old-bossy self, only moving a little slower. "I hope you can cook, Penny, because I'm not allowing staff inside the house ever again. No maid, no cook, no—"

"I don't know how to cook!" I protested.

"You can Wiki it or something—because I like to eat."

"You're sexist. How come Nate doesn't have to cook?"

"Nate can cook. I just liked the image of you scurrying around the kitchen in a skimpy little apron. Maybe cleaning the house in a tiny French maid outfit…"

"Now we're talking," Nate said with a poke to my thigh.

"Fuck you both," I spat out.

"You *will*, princess, very soon. And don't forget I'm still well enough to spank your fine ass if you can't control your tongue."

"I control my tongue *just fine*," I flirted.

"Well, that I'd like to see again soon," he winked.

Nate's arm continued to heal as we cared for Rex. I controlled the meds, which Nate never questioned. We took turns night and day ensuring Rex was taken care of, and yes, I did cook. A week after we brought him home, Rex asked me to cut his meds in half, and then a few days later, to cut them entirely. He had some pain as his body adjusted to being off the heavy opiates, but he fought through it.

One afternoon, a few days after going off the meds, Rex called me into his room. With a pat he motioned for me to sit next to him on the bed. "Hey sweetheart, you asked me about calling your father. My brain has been muddled, but is that something you still want to do?"

"Yes," I answered eagerly. "I'm sure he's been a worried wreck…"

"Just realize he doesn't know anything more than that you ran off with Nathaniel Slater on a getaway. Us *taking* you, I'd rather you skip that part."

"I-I hadn't thought about that. You don't think he'd understand why you did it? He should know about the—"

He shook his head and placed his hand on my knee. "No, Penny, he wouldn't understand. Your father would love to use that as an excuse to harm me. We have some history, he and I. That's one of the reasons I freaked when Nate took you. That's why they tried to hire me to kill his daughter."

"History?"

"Princess, I haven't gone into it because I know you love your father. But…he's deep into the drug cartels here, laundering their money. I, well I was on the other side of that, trying to bring him down. He wouldn't know who Roger Renton is, but he sure as hell will go ape shit if you mention Rex in Colombia, get my drift?"

I sat silently. It was hard for me to accept that my father was a criminal, but I knew it was true. "Do you think my mother knew?" I said barely above a whisper.

"I don't know." He rubbed my knee, waiting for me to absorb the truth about my father.

"I'll call him, but leave you out of it."

"Use the phone in my office—the black one. Dial this code first," he wrote some numbers on a notepad and handed it to me. "It'll make the line untraceable."

I took the paper with the cryptic numbers into Rex's office and picked up the black phone on his desk. I keyed in the sequence of numbers, and after an odd dial tone, dialed my father's cell number. He picked up on the fourth ring.

"Dad? It's Penny."

"Penelope, where the fuck are you?"

"Oh, I—I'm in…I'm with Nate Slater, do you remember him?"

"Yeah, good luck with that. He's way out of your league. He'll dump you faster than a hand of Blackjack."

Same old Dad. "Well, we're together now. I plan to stay with him, unless you…"

"No, that's great. Spend his money instead of mine. It'll keep you out of my hair until he tires of you and tosses you back. Good luck, I guess."

"Dad, um, is there any way you can have someone send my passport and stuff to me?"

"I'll have them pack up all of your shit, Penelope. Hospitality could really use your penthouse to comp whales with. Where do you want your belongings sent?"

"Uh," I paused. I couldn't have it sent here. "His father's house in Wilson, North Carolina. I think I have the address here, can you hang on a sec…"

"We'll 411 it." He was quiet for a moment before adding, "I hope you're happy with him, Penny. I really do."

"Thanks, Dad, I will be. I love you."

"Love ya, too. Gotta go, there's trouble on the floor. Some freaking autistic card counter is cleaning out the house. We'll talk soon, okay?"

"Yeah, Dad, sure thing." The line went dead.

Chapter Seventeen

"Are you sure you're ready?" I asked him.

"Oh, baby, I'm more than ready—I'm about to explode. I *need* you."

Rex had been home from the hospital for a while, and he was healing fast. Because the wound was abdominal, he hadn't had sex other than a few strained blowjobs. Nate and I felt guilty, but not guilty enough not to fuck like rabbits whenever the recovering Rex wasn't around. While eating dinner, cooked by Nate, Rex called us out on our sneaky sex. As he popped a meatball into his mouth, he asked, "When do I get back in on all the fucking that's going around?"

"Fucking?" Nate asked, his cheeks blushing in a guilty tell.

"Cut the shit, I get it. But I'm ready to re-join civilization."

We both smiled wide—we'd missed him. Nate sipped his wine and answered, "Well, King Rex, let's finish this food and wander over to Threesome Land."

"Which position? I mean I don't want to put any pressure on the incision—and the pull from when you—" I was looking at the shirtless Rex, the long cut from his surgery was almost fully healed, but inside there was still some pain.

"Fuck, Penny, cut out the clinical shit! It's not turning me on. I want to be a man again, not a damn patient!"

"I'm sorry," I whispered, my voice as sultry as I could manage. I slid my hands across his chest and around his broad back. "I want you so badly—I just worry about hurting you."

"Let me worry about that, okay?" His lips brushed mine—the electric charge igniting from my tongue to my clit as he pulled me closer. "You are *so* beautiful," he said into my ear. "I'm not waiting for Nate," he breathed, slowly undressing me until I stood naked in front of him. My hands reached for his belt, pulling it from his jeans as I grappled for his fly. "*It's been so long… I need you inside me,*" I moaned as I freed his hefty erection from the worn jeans. "I love you so much, Penny." He stepped from the jeans and leaned back on the bed, my eager body following to straddle his wide hips. "This okay?" I asked, still nervous to hurt him. "It's perfect," he groaned as I sank onto him, my pussy straining to stretch quickly enough to take his full length. My lips found his as Nate, back from cleaning up dinner, undressed and crept behind me—his silky naked skin brushing against my ass as I was filled by Rex.

"I love you, Penelope," Nate's velvety voice said into my ear from behind. I leaned back to kiss him, torturing Rex beneath me with my stillness. "Do you want my cock or my tongue back here?" Nate growled as his cock lurched at the crack of my ass. "I want you to fuck me—I want you both at the same time." Rex's teased cock lurched inside of me—I'd never taken them together like that.

Nate reached over toward the bottle of lube and slicked both of us up. "Tell me if it's too much, babe," Nate said as he positioned himself at my back entrance. "*Fuck*," I moaned as he slid slowly into me. The sensation of being stretched by both of them was more intense than I'd ever imagined. The sexual satisfaction of being filled by them I expected, but I didn't expect the emotion of the three of us being physically joined, so close, so intimate, to be so completely overwhelming that I felt tears spring to my eyes.

"Are you okay, baby? Does that hurt?" Rex's deep baritone asked, his palm cradling my cheek. Nate stopped moving until I answered. "I-I'm perfect," I answered, "I just love you both so much." He exhaled in relief, his long arms reaching along my sides to clasp Nate's strong thighs as Nate began to thrust again from behind. We made love for the next hour, three lovers tangled into each other, my body the conduit between the hearts and bodies of the two finest men I've ever known. That night, and many others just like it, I knew I was the luckiest girl on earth.

Chapter Eighteen

"So things have changed?" My question hung in the air like a puff of smoke. I sat across from the somber Rex in a café in Bogotá. Nate was down the street shopping for some computer part he needed. The air was humid and thick, the beginning of Colombian summer bearing down.

He took a slow sip from his steaming mug of black coffee, swallowing as if savoring a sip of fine bourbon. "I'm not sure when it happened, but it happened. I *want* him, like I want you—in that way. At least, when you're there, the lines are blurred."

We'd been locked together in bliss since Rex came home—the three of us in love, oblivious to the morals and standards of the world back home. Rex had allowed Nate to express his feelings physically, but always through oral sex. The night before, however, had been different.

We'd come to the city two days prior to spend a weekend away from the remote compound we called home. Rex indulged us with an urban break—restaurants, bars, shopping, and maid service. Nate and I loved life on King Rex Island, but we were also young city-dwellers at heart, and Bogotá was the sort of eclectic melting pot of chaos that he knew we'd enjoy. Rex merely tolerated it, but did enjoy watching us cavort like carefree young adults.

The night prior, Nate and I spent the evening partying at a hot local dance club. Rex refused to go with us. "Loud, smoky bars just aren't my thing," he said when I whined for him to join us. When we got back from a night of grinding our bodies for hours on the sticky dance floor, Rex was waiting up in a large side chair, his usual tumbler of whiskey in his right hand. "I wish you'd have been there," I said to him as I wiped off my eye makeup. "I wanted to grind my hips between the two sexiest men in Colombia." Nate unbuttoned his shirt as Rex looked up from some book he was reading—a hard cover, written in Spanish.

"He can't dance, Pen," Nate said as he unfastened the heavy Rolex from around his wrist.

"What the fuck? Of course I can dance." Rex stood up from his chair.

"This is news to me," Nate said with a shrug.

"It's Colombia, for fuck's sake—my hips don't lie!"

Nate and I groaned at Rex's tired Shakira reference, but he ignored us and walked to the center of the large hotel suite, kicking an oversized velvet ottoman to the side. He held up his right hand to me in a classic, "Shall we dance?" pose.

I shook my head no, fighting peals of laughter. "I can't… I'll pee my pants!"

He pointed his scolding index finger at me, before turning to the blushing Nate.

"Scared?" he taunted, adding, "Can the pretty boy cut a rug?"

"Oh my God!" I squealed, snorting like a teenager.

"This is messed *up*," Nate said through his laughter, walking toward Rex.

"I'm not talking about that gyrating shit you did at the club. I mean actual moves!"

"What music do you want?" I asked. Nate's hand was in Rex's raised right one, their arms laced around each other's waists. Seeing their bodies so close, my mood went from amused to downright horny.

"On my phone there's a Latin dance playlist—just pick any of those." Rex's eyes never left Nate's, their bodies so close I could barely concentrate on the music. My eyes wandered to where their crotches touched. With a click on Rex's phone, the lyrical tones of a song named *Tango Al Dente* poured from the device. "Let me lead," Rex said quietly to Nate as he twisted his hips. "I always do," Nate flirted, his lean body flawlessly mimicking the swerving motion of Rex's torso.

One foot, then the other, and within seconds my men were gliding across the floor, Nate effortlessly keeping up with Rex's fluid tango moves. Their bodies melded together as one as they moved—large, masculine, and sensually intertwined. I fell onto the overstuffed sofa in the living room of the hotel suite, watching them dance and craving them so badly I could feel the moisture soak my lace panties.

The music ended and the men stopped moving, but didn't let go of each other. Rex held Nate close, cheek to cheek, for several long moments before they reluctantly parted. "That was epic," Nate breathed as he sank into the sofa next to me. I fell into him. "I loved that," I sighed. I reached down to pull off my stilettos, rubbing my feet from the long night of dancing.

Rex knelt down in front of me, his strong fingers taking over as he massaged my feet. "So next time, I'll pick the place and we'll do *that* kind of dancing—deal?"

"Deal," we both answered without hesitation.

"I'm going to bed," Rex said, stepping out of his shoes and walking toward the bedroom. "First one in here is getting fucked."

I looked at Nate, my eyes wide. "Go!" I urged.

"He didn't mean it, babe. He won't even *really* kiss me."

"But what if…?" I raised an eyebrow, the thought driving me wild with need.

I'd noticed Rex getting more and more sexual with Nate. There'd been more touching, a growing physical closeness ever since he'd come home from the hospital. Change was in the air, and I could sense it whether they did or not.

"Come on, let's go together," I said, reaching for Nate's hand.

Rex stood naked next to the bed—a bottle of his favorite lube placed on the duvet as Nate and I walked in together arm in arm.

"Ah, a tie," he said. "Good plan…good for me, anyway. Strip and do it quickly."

He pointed to the plush green carpet. "On your knees, both of you," he commanded. It was typical for Rex to begin with Nate and I kneeled in front of him, pleasuring him with our mouths, either one at a time or together. It had become standard Rex foreplay, two eager tongues lavishing attention on the giant cock they adored. But tonight, Rex ended the tongue bath quickly, directing me to lie on my back on the edge of the bed.

He deftly removed all of the metal piercing the shaft of his cock except the one along the ridge underneath—I'd never seen him take that one out. I asked him why once, and he simply answered, "It feels too fucking good."

"Lick her," he said to Nate, casually pointing to my flooded pussy. I spread my legs wide as Nate's talented tongue drove me to the brink of orgasm. Rex removing the metal meant he had plans for my ass— but he usually only did that after I'd come several times.

Nate's tongue drove me to ecstasy as Rex hovered over me from the side, his teeth pulling a nipple as I groaned and struggled for more. I was in heaven, two mouths and twenty fingers licking, fucking, sucking, pulling, and kissing overwhelmed me with carnal pleasure until I begged them to stop— my release so complete it exhausted me.

"Fuck her. Hard." Rex barked at Nate.

I was still shuddering from my climax when Nate's long cock pounded into me, time and time again. Rex knelt on the bed behind him, spreading the slippery lube over his thick cock as he watched. Nate stopped thrusting, burying himself deep inside me as Rex leaned over his strong back to kiss me. Our three faces were touching as Rex's tongue slid across mine.

Nate groaned as Rex bit my lower lip. I could feel the movement, but Nate wasn't thrusting—Rex was...into Nate.

Rex's lips didn't leave mine as he slid his well-lubed hardness into Nate, an erotic moan from Nate vibrating across my chest. The moment was too hot— I had to watch. I pulled back from Rex's kiss, my view obscured by Nate lying on top of me, his throbbing cock impaling me. With both large hands, Rex spread Nate wide, slamming into his virgin ass with more force than he'd ever fucked me with.

Nate's face rose to mine, his cock resuming its punishing thrust into my clenching pussy. His steel-blue eyes misted over with lust as he sank his sharp teeth into the side of my neck, bringing me to yet another thundering orgasm. Rex pulled him up by his shoulders, wrenching Nate's bite from the delicate skin of my throat. "Watch," Rex snapped at me. Nate hovered over me, his cock hard and slick from our shared arousal. I leaned up the best I could with Nate's heavy torso braced across mine, watching as Rex fucked him. Hard, then agonizingly slow, the rhythm changing as he edged both of their climaxes. The look in both of their eyes was pure desire—Rex wasn't just giving Nate what he wanted, he was fucking him because he craved it, too.

With one hand pulling back on Nate's shoulder to keep him raised from me, Rex's other large hand reached around to fist Nate's long cock, stroking him in rhythm to his own thrusts into Nate's backside. "*Fuck*," Nate howled as he came, the creamy seed coating my chest.

"Lick it up," Rex growled. Nate's hungry tongue lapped at my breasts as Rex exploded in orgasm, collapsing over Nate's back in a sexual dog-pile of the three of us, exhausted, our hearts and bodies wondrously wrapped together as one.

"Why can't I go with you?" Rex was dressing to go into the city. It had been two weeks since we'd been to Bogotá for the weekend, and we'd had so much fun I yearned to go back. The memory of Rex inside of Nate for the first time that weekend was still my favorite fantasy, even though since that night they'd been together in that way several times.

He finished buttoning up a dark linen shirt. He'd given up his trademark black t-shirts in favor of button ups to go over the wound dressings. Now, he was fully healed and back to wearing his soft t-shirts— except for today. "Penny," he turned toward me and took me into his arms, "I know you're going stir crazy cooped up here. I promise we'll go into the city again next week, okay? The three of us. But today...I need to go alone because I'm working on a surprise." I nuzzled up toward his neck, standing on my tiptoes to reach him. "I love surprises," I said before planting a kiss as high as I could reach.

"Good. Behave, and I should be able to show you tonight."

"I will. Nate's supposed to teach me that funky pressure point stuff and some other defense thing."

"Oh shit, I'm in trouble," he teased, rubbing the tip of his nose against mine.

"I love you." I missed him already.

"I love you more than anything, baby."

The new driver, Samuel, interrupted our kiss, and with a quick wave, Rex was gone.

By the time he came home, it was dark. Nate and I were cuddled up on the sofa in the living room, marathon watching our favorite Netflix shows. Rex knelt down in front of us, blocking the blue glow of the television screen. "I need to talk to the two of you," he said, his face somber. My heart froze as we followed him to the kitchen, where he flicked on the overhead light. "Sit," he commanded, pointing to the bar stools.

"Okay, this won't be easy for me," he paced in front of us. "I don't do mush, but I need to get this out." We both nodded, Nate's hand reaching for mine.

Rex began to slowly unbutton his shirt. "So these unfortunate bullet holes pretty much fucked up my artwork, as you know. So, I went to my tattoo gal today and got some patchwork done."

"Did you get Evelyn's name removed?" After the shooting, I nagged him to get her name taken off and also to stop wearing his gold wedding band. All I managed to get out of him was, "Let me think about it."

He took a deep breath. "No, Princess. I've thought about it, but let me explain. The ring," he held up his *right* hand, "I had it resized today to wear on this finger. Maybe someday I'll wear a different one on my left ring finger," he shot us both a warm grin. "But, the ring is a big part of my past, and it's a good reminder to me to never, ever let love come last again. As far as the tattoos, this is the story of my life," he dropped the shirt to the ground. "The good *and* the bad, they are all lessons to me. I did, however, make an addition today." My eyes went to the bandage across his midsection, just above the *Trust* tattoo. With a slight grimace he pulled it off. It was red, wrapped it some sort of cellophane looking tape, but we were there. I blinked hard to try to see through the fountain of tears that clouded my eyes.

"I can't believe it," I whispered in awe.

"It has to heal, it'll look better, don't worry…"

Nate was frozen in his seat, his hand gripping mine so tightly I was losing circulation. "You didn't have to…I mean you already…for me…" Nate couldn't put words together. He gulped and managed to get out, "I never thought you'd do that for *me.*"

I wiped the tears away with the back of my hand. In the same script as the word *Trust*, *Penelope* and *Nathaniel* were intertwined with the Roman numeral for *three*. "It's beautiful, thank you." He walked toward us. "You're so damn sappy—I'll be bitching tomorrow about how badly it itches—such fucking long names." Nate pulled me up from my stool and we fell into Rex, who gave an overly dramatic, "Ow!" as we selfishly examined the fresh tattoo.

"Thank you," Nate whispered, his fingers tracing the letters of his name as Rex winced.

I placed a palm on each man's cheek. "You two complete me," I said, the words cliché, but I meant them. Nate's lips fell onto mine, the comforting embrace of Rex's arms wrapped around us both. Nate and I broke our kiss when Rex spoke. "I love you both more than life," he said as his deep blue eyes misted over.

Rex leaned in, lowering his quivering lips to mine. I loved him so much at that moment that I could barely focus. He kissed me, warm and loving, for what felt like forever—I never wanted his lips to leave mine. When we parted, he gave me a warm smile before turning his loving gaze to Nate. Despite the sexual closeness they'd discovered, Rex had yet to kiss Nate the way he kissed me. I expected him to maybe say something to Nate, possibly give him a hair ruffle or a peck on the forehead, but what happened next caused tears to pour down my cheeks. Rex kissed him—long, intimate, and without reserve. Kissing both men was spiritual for me, but seeing them kiss each other—hard jaws, scruffy five-o-clock shadows, strong lips melding together bound us as three in ways I could never have imagined.

After the kiss, Rex held up his left hand, three fingers splayed out at us. "Three," he said. "We are three. I love you both."

I reached up three fingers and held them to Rex's. "Three, I love you both," I repeated.

Nate gulped hard before holding up three fingers from his left hand to ours and repeated the words that I knew would become an oath between us for the rest of our lives—"Three, I love you both." A joyous tear slid down my cheek as nine fingers intertwined in an unbreakable bond that exists to this day. Love finds a way to thrive—defying all labels, crashing through all boundaries, forgiving and mending the pain of the past.

We are three, and we love each other. Nothing else matters—we have found our own version of true love, and for the three of us, it's perfect.

Word-of-mouth is crucial for any author to succeed. If you enjoyed this book, please leave a review on Amazon. Even if it were just a sentence or two, it would make all the difference and be very much appreciated.

Be sure to follow my website www.sjdhunt.com for updates on upcoming releases, bonus material, and *Aunt Kitty's Prudish Erotica*.

Also by Sam J.D. Hunt

The Thomas Hunt Series:
Roulette: Love Is A Losing Game
Blackjack: Wicked Game
Poker: Foolish Games

DEEP: A Captive Tale
The Hunt for Eros

With Thomas Hunt:
Dagger: American Fighter Pilot

Titles available for Kindle, Kindle Unlimited, and Paperback.

Keep in Touch with Sam:

Amazon: www.amazon.com/author/samhunt
Facebook: http://www.facebook.com/SJDHunt
Twitter: @sjd_hunt
Google+: google.com/+SamJDHunt
Pinterest:www.pinterest.com/sjd_hunt/
Goodreads:
https://www.goodreads.com/SJD_Hunt

Acknowledgements

Thank you to my loving family for giving me the time and space to write this novel as quickly as it flowed out. Rex, Nate, and Penny absorbed me, and I'll always be grateful for their patience. Thanks also to the core group of ladies who tirelessly promote my work for free; Hunts' Hustlers, led by Ashley Carr and Missy Harton, and including Jenny Shepherd, Jessica Cecconi, Kelly Mallett, Laura Frasher, Melissa Aguirre, Reva Coomer, and Tina England, who also beta read for me for this book and provided valuable feedback early in the process, as did Daphne Caldwell.

To my last-minute volunteer editors for giving the book a final once-over, Kelly Mallett and Missy Borucki. Thank you to Laura Frasher, for fielding the book world as my loyal right-hand for so long. I'd also like to thank my ARC readers and the fabulous blogs who support indie writing, and especially erotica. Without the support of my fan group, Hunt's Hideaway, it would have been a lonely year—I'm so happy to know each of you. Last, but not least, to my readers who have continued to support me as I tell wild stories and strive to improve my craft and find my voice.

Made in the USA
Middletown, DE
28 March 2016